The Case of the
With

(A W

By Donnie Rust

ISBN-10 – 1982014202

ISBN-13 – 978-1982014209

I would like to state that everything that follows is all absolutely true.

— *Donnie Rust.*

For my little octopus.

1.

I frowned and put the iPad onto the desk.

"Centaurs," I said.

"Is that a question?" my assistant Danielle asked, diligently placing a mug of tepid coffee onto a cork placemat. The coffee inside was brewed until it could have been carved into a Christmas decoration. Drinking it was as close as a beverage could get to kicking you in the teeth but I had waited too long to tell her that it wasn't how I liked my coffee. I had said latte and she had instead just brought my coffee three quarters of an hour after I asked for it. Now she thought she was doing a good job and I didn't have the heart to tell her otherwise, because, frankly, she scared me a little.

"I suppose it could be," I ventured. "We have *centaurs* in Norwich?"

"Oh yes," she said, wrinkling her nose in distaste. "Horrible, horrible halfies."

"Halfies?" I asked.

She gave me a severe look, which looked scathing despite her having the height and slight stature of a fairytale character; it was something in those slender eyebrows and those piercing ethereal blue eyes. "You do know that they are half horse and half man, yes?"

I had a vague recollection of seeing something about them. "So they're not half breeds?"

"No," Danielle said, her expression shifting to accommodate the outrageousness of such a thing. "That would mean that a horse would have had to have had sex with a human. They can't do that, Mr Ambassador... they are *different* species after all."

I rolled my eyes, realising that, like any political position, people naturally assumed I was a keystone that was meant to just be the right shape. In simpler terms, it meant everyone assumed I was an idiot.

"You don't seem to like them," I pointed out, looking at the write-up on the iPad.

"They are brutish," she said. "When they first arrived in the city they caused some trouble. A gang of them destroyed the kebab shop on Brodella Street because they were selling horse meat."

"Were they arrested?"

"The centaurs were," Danielle pointed out.

"No, I meant the owners of the kebab shop. Horse meat is illegal now."

She took her iPad from me and made a note. "I will find out. But your job isn't to police Norwich," she said, her youthful voice contrasting the tone she applied.

I shrugged and lied – "I am well aware of my responsibilities, thank you. Okay, so what is the issue with the centaurs?"

She handed me the iPad. "It's all there."

"Give me the summarised version," I said, waving away the pad and taking up her coffee. I chewed thoughtfully on it while she spoke.

"There is some background information that you may need to fully understand," she surmised.

"I have a very busy day, so let's hurry up," I said. But the truth was that Danielle controlled my diary, so of the two of us, she knew this better than me.

"The centaurs are a fighting race and measure themselves by their ability to do combat," she began. "Everything for them is a sign of strength; they believe that weakness should be destroyed at the onset and from the moment of birth every one of them is tested. They value war so much that when they're not involved in their own

7

battles they will happily join in others, and have participated in a number of human wars."

"I didn't know that was allowed?"

"Humans don't see what is in front of them," she pointed out – I wondered if she remembered that I was technically still human but she continued. "Because of these wars they are very well regarded by a number of international leaders. They are a valuable fighting force – revered even, if not feared, and because they prefer to stay away from other human affairs they are tolerated. Norwich and a few Late cities offer a free area for them. Mostly the Otherwise stay away from them too and the Lost can't find them. Their greatest warrior and leader visited the city last week. Aggregosh."

"Bless you," I said.

"No," Danielle said. "His name was Aggregosh."

"Was?"

"He was killed last night," she said, pointing at the iPad to emphasise that it was all written down for me.

How many Ambassadors do you know who are involved in the front line investigations of murders and killings? Now you know one at least.

"Who is investigating?" I asked, standing up and buttoning my jacket.

She didn't look up. "You are."

I sat down again.

"What?" she asked.

"I'm not an investigator, I'm an Ambassador," I said.

"You know that you are whatever they need you to be," she said. "*You* chose the word Ambassador because you thought it sounded catchy."

I looked my personal assistant directly in the eyes. She was an elf, of sorts, standing a little over five foot, and had a figure so lithe and pixie-ish I was constantly expecting her to be blown away by the breeze of a book closing. Her dark hair was hung in a sweeping mop around her head so that it hid the way her ears stuck out. Her small nose and small chin were in perfect proportion and her eyes, which were *just* slightly too large, were one of the few tells that revealed her species. That and that she could fit more judgement into a single word than almost any other creature... "catchy" had been transformed into a lengthy and scathing insult.

"Will the city council be investigating at all?"

"One of the council will be investigating," Danielle said.

"Oh? Why didn't you mention? Who is it?"

"You."

I closed my eyes and counted to ten.

"If you will insist on clenching your jaw you should wear a gumshield," she said.

I envisioned putting the little elf over my knee and tanning her hide with my hand, but put it aside and said. "Fine... call me a cab will you?"

2.

Like teenage lovers, autumn entered winter without any grace or style, but rather a sudden and unexpected blast with shards. Due to the nature of the city's topography, the change in the seasons was anything but reliable. Unable to reach all areas at the same time, it meant that seasons lingered in some places for longer, which was why such a wide selection of Lost, Late, or Otherwise were able to make their homes here. If you needed an environment hot and muggy all year round, without being a country known for all year round mugginess, there was a corner of Norwich that would be perfect for you. Or if you preferred all year Arctic conditions, Norwich had that in wealth.

It was the last days of November. The first few inches of snow had fallen and brought the city to a standstill. Main roads had become parking lots and wrapped up pedestrians moved through the streets like cattle, slowly oozing into shops and market stalls searching for Christmas presents and warmer clothing.

I was playing noughts and crosses in the condensation of the taxi's window while Danielle spoke on the cell phone by my side, populating my diary and my calendar.

The taxi driver, who was from one of the firms exclusively used by the Late of Norwich, had managed to find the few connected roads that were free of traffic, having been forgotten by those who were not Late. Due to this, he had passed through several different weather systems, but at that moment was driving through a strip of road surrounded by white snow-laden fields. The road was grey like the parting in the fur of a polar bear. I could see light blue mountains in the far distance.

"Please don't do that," the driver said over his shoulder. "I'll just have to clean your grubby fingerprints off my window when you get out."

"And you are a public official," Danielle reminded me without looking up.

I withdrew my finger and sat glumly.

"Don't often get fares to the horses," the driver said. He was a weathered old man, whose neck was so slender it looked about to break under the weight of his bald head. But there was a grizzliness to him that I liked – he added, "Lovely countryside though."

"When was the last fare?" I asked.

"Crikey," he said. "Let me think. Probably about fifteen, maybe sixteen years ago?"

"You've been driving for a while then?"

"Ages," he admitted. "Know Norwich like the back of my hand."

"What else is out in these parts?" I asked.

These parts, while for hundreds of miles in every direction all I could see was a flat land of white with gnarled shapes sticking out of it and fresh snow falling like curtains connecting land and cloud. It was scrunched. An element of the Norwich topography, great spaces of land like this were technically crushed together and folded. It meant that this whole landscape of desolation was fitted neatly into a courtyard or those convenient gaps between houses that provide shortcuts for cats and youths fleeing the police. Between a hundred and a thousand miles to my left there was probably a neighbour leaning out her window talking to a neighbour a similar distance away from my right.

"Well," the driver said, "you have centaurs, obviously, they love these open plains.

Chupacabra roam them too – I wouldn't advise you to go for a walk. A couple of vestibin, a winchikari or two. I heard there was a tribe of Needlemen who trained out in these parts. Why? You paying them all a visit or I could add a tour to your trip if you like?"

"No thank you," Danielle leaned in. "We need to go directly to the centaurs."

I closed my mouth then asked her, "Are you my personal assistant or my manager?"

"What is the difference?" she asked.

"I... well, wages I guess."

"You don't pay me," she said curtly. "A fact that was specified so that you don't ever think about doing something inappropriate."

I swallowed and looked out the window a tad guiltily. A vast tide of bruise coloured clouds was approaching from the west. "How long until we get to the centaurs?"

"Oh we'll be there in about five minutes or so," the driver said, swerving around a pothole. "Do you want me to wait for you while I'm there?"

"Yes," Danielle said, adding to me, "There are a couple of appointments for this afternoon but nothing for a couple of hours. How much time do you think you'll need at the scene?"

"How the hell should I know?" I asked.

"It was all written down," she began.

"I read the write-up, their leader has been killed; assassinated. I'm going in there to find out who did it – if it was obvious who did it I wouldn't be needed, so the report you wrote up is helpful, but not as much as you think."

"You will be able to help though, yes?" she asked.

I shrugged. "I'm not a detective."

3.

The taxi driver pulled into the mouth of a dirt track that led away from the main road and told us, "I'll be waiting here. I can't take you guys down there I'm afraid." As I started to get out he said, "I bet you wish you'd worn something less fancy."

My suit shoes skidded over the layer of packed ice on the road and the cold stabbed through my thin Ted Baker trousers. On cue, a wind tore up my overcoat and flung it around me.

I held the door open for Danielle, who climbed out and pulled the collar of her black coat close to her jaw, but didn't seem nearly as affected by the weather as I was. I closed the taxi door and did a quick take of our surroundings. At all hours of the clock the land was a clear horizon line, as flat as a tabletop and covered with white snow and ice. In the far distance were those grey mountain tops, but aside from that the wind was able to gather a bit of pace and, with a strong run up, hit us like an avalanche of frozen bricks. Directly in front of us the dirt road stretched away to a distant encampment made up of a number of tall tepees and a welcoming column of smoke.

Having been trampled out by the hoof-falls of hundreds of centaurs, the road was pitted and uneven, with many frozen puddles just waiting to take full advantage of my city shoes.

It took half an hour for us to make it only halfway up the road. My feet were soaking wet and numb, my suit splattered up one side with road water and the tips of my fingers were on fire with chill. My concern for my personal assistant evaporated very quickly as it was obvious I was having more problems than she. I had asked her once or twice, "You okay?" and she would look at me from where she was standing as if she'd just stepped out of a salon and nod with a pleasant smile.

She's absolutely loving this, I thought glumly as I stepped onto another slab of ice that turned out to be thinner than I had planned and plunged my foot into the dark, mucky waters beneath. I extricated my foot and stood balancing on one leg while watching my toes wriggling in a wet sock for a moment before trying to get my shoe out of the puddle.

"-ucking puddles," I grumbled under my breath as another blast of wind licked up under the back of my shirt and tore it up away from my skin.

Cold and wet. There is no better way to make a person feel spectacularly dreary and depressed. I was so cold I had stopped shivering. My ears were ablaze from the cold and the tip of my nose stung.

"They're not puddles," Danielle informed me.

"Huh?" I asked, wriggling my foot back into a sodden shoe.

"They are hoof prints."

I looked at the size of the puddle for a while.

"You have never seen a centaur, have you?" she asked.

"Half man, half horse," I said. "Greek myth."

"The Greek myth comes from horsemen being seen on the horizon," Danielle told me. "In the silhouette the two look like one creature. But they were people riding horses and it's an effect of the eyes, like how a corgi can look like a wolf if it throws the right shadow. If the centaurs were half horse, it wouldn't be any horse you would want to ride."

Carefully I lowered my foot until it was just above the dark water and took a measure of the size of the puddle compared to my own foot. I smiled.

"You are fearless?" she asked.

"Oh no," I said, shoving my hands into my coat pockets and trudging onwards. "But the bigger they are, the bigger their fire will be."

Anything could have happened during the remainder of the walk. When you're cold, wet and miserable you just don't notice anything that's happening around you because you know you couldn't deal with it. By the time we reached the first of the tepees all I was interested in was finding the source of that smoke.

We were expected; that was obvious by the way none of the centaurs attacked us when we arrived. But it was later that I reflected on the experience of seeing my first horse-man. The tepees, made out of animal hide, were huge. Each one was at least three stories high and secured with a netting of ropes and giant pegs, each with a hammered top that was as flat and as large as a stool. The hides of the tepees were light tan and flapped audibly in the wind. As we entered the circumference of the camp, where the road took on a far more mushy and wet feel, for every step I had to hook my toes inside my shoes to stop them from being sucked off my feet. This was a concern until the flaps of the first tents were flung open and I saw my very first centaur.

"Don't stare," Danielle said urgently.

I am six feet five inches tall. I am broad shouldered and have to duck under doorways to not hit my head. I have also worked very hard to add a particular width to my shoulders and I tower over my fellow man, but felt like a rodent in comparison to what stepped out of that tent.

Twice my height to its shoulder, the beast that trotted out of the tepee was far removed from the graceful and beautiful creatures of legend that I had seen in picture books. So many details struck me at once – the astonishing width of the upper body, the boulder shoulders, the neck so thick it looked corded with steel cables. Its lower body, if it had been compared to any animal, looked more like a giant wolf with huge, mud-encrusted hooves. Danielle was correct; you'd never try to ride something that packed with muscle. It would have been like using a saddle made of potatoes.

I would also not describe its upper body as being human either. It was its own beast, a six limbed creature with arms that were twice the size of my legs with hands that could have crushed wheelbarrows as if they were coke cans. Long braids were tied back from its wide forehead. Hair trailed from its lower body up to its shoulders and a sketch-work of scars had left its flesh with the texture of rope.

It carried a spear the length of a canoe in one hand, black lengths of fabric woven into the binding at its head.

"You are staring," Danielle said.

And I wasn't watching where I was going either.

"Oh bollocks!"

From out of the tepees more of the community trotted out, all massive and terrifying and they all looked at me with the kind of disdain and disinterest you would give a plate of food when you weren't hungry. The mud gave a sucking sound as I pulled my face out of it and when I clambered into a sitting position I tried to think of a way to salvage some of my dignity.

"You *really* need to get up," Danielle said.

I looked up at her, noticing with not a small amount of exasperation that she was still perfectly clean and did not seem at all concerned about the growing number of giant horse people who were gathering around, tall enough to create a wind breaker against the biting weather with a particular odour that illustrated how little they cared about personal hygiene.

"I'm just taking a moment," I said, wiping mud from my face. "Just taking a moment in the mud."

"This *isn't* mud," she said through her teeth.

The forest of legs to my right and just behind parted and a particularly large centaur marched in. He bore the air of someone in charge, this being the look of someone accustomed to winning fights.

"Who are you?" he demanded in a voice slightly slurred by the fangs.

I introduced myself and Danielle. "And you are?"

"I am in charge," he said. "My name is Gregore."

"Pleasure to meet you," I said, getting up. I didn't offer my hand in greeting. It seemed a silly thing to do seeing as in one hand he held a spear that had various skulls hanging off the shaft and in the other he held what I assumed was the remains of his last meal. It looked like it had tried to give a fight.

"Pleasure is for breeding," he grunted. "We condone your presence only because we are nomads to this land and wish to abide by the laws, but you will leave as soon as your business is concluded." He turned and walked away, clearing a path in the crowd, and said over his shoulder, "I would suggest you reach your conclusions sooner rather than later."

The crowd dispersed, having designated us as not for combat, and we followed Gregore. With relief he appeared to be taking us directly to the column of smoke, which proved to belong to a gigantic bonfire with flames the size of a house around which the centaurs stood with their spears pointed into the flames with wet chunks of sizzling meat on the end of them. Nearby the pillar posts of the ribcage of a giant animal were being scraped for meat by smaller female centaurs. The smell of cooking meat filled the air and the fire had left the ground steaming. I paid particular attention to the centaur females' breasts.

Gregore led us around the fire, and as he spoke his voice boomed, but at most I was staring at his horse's ass as he dropped out some significant droppings which I danced around to avoid.

"We found Aggregosh in the morning," he explained. "In his tent. He was assassinated."

"What makes you think this?" I asked.

"He did not fight."

He led us to a tepee with an uncommonly closed flap. It was the largest in the camp, rising out of the others like a pyramid. The centaur came to a stop outside. "He is still inside..." he said. "We have not disturbed the scene."

"Thank you," I said. "Before we go in I do have some questions. After you found him what did you do?"

"Contacted the city council and asked them to investigate," Gregore said stiffly. "We want to go to war over this so it is important that we know who to kill."

"Do you have any enemies?" I asked.

"Is that a legitimate question?" he asked, cocking an eyebrow.

"Consider that one answered then," I said. "Finally, did anyone go into the tent prior to this? Was Aggregosh alone?"

"We do not know," Gregore said. He pulled the hide flap aside and gestured with a jerk of his head that we were to enter. "Make your investigation. We will await your determinations."

Danielle and I stepped into the muggy warmth of the tent and the flap fell shut behind us.

"He sounds adamant," I commented.

"He is. Our findings here will result in all-out war," she said. "What you find here is going to be directing the first cannon. So to speak."

I smiled. "I work best under pressure."

"Really?" she asked incredulously. "That's not what I've heard."

Immediately to my left was a spear, similar in size and style to Gregore's but with more skulls. Otherwise the inside of the tent was void of any furniture, beaten down earth wrapped around a wide central pole of hardened red wood. I recognised the wood from the forests bordering the eastern boundary of the city. The wood was harder than steel.

Behind it, sprawled in the dirt, was the body of Aggregosh.

Danielle doubled over and heaved at the sight of it.

"You okay?" I asked, walking away from her to the recently deceased centaur leader.

"I'm... not good with... dead bodies," she managed.

"Just stay there then," I cautioned. "It's worse up close."

Another heave. I hid my smile.

The centaur leader was definitely a fighter. Even in death he looked ready for a scrap. He lay on his back, two of his hooved legs almost airborne, his lower hooves dug into the dirt. His upper half was sprawled, his insanely muscular and scarred arms spread out, the mane of his hair spread out behind his brutish face. His dark eyes blankly stared at the ceiling and his dry tusked mouth hung open in a cry of utter horror. The reason for the facial expression was probably linked to the way in which he had died.

"Are you able to make notes?" I asked.

"Um…" Danielle managed, retching some more.

"Put that iPad onto voice recording for me and try to keep your puking down," I said.

With her back turned and one elbow on her knee she held the pad out to the side.

"You sure that will work?" I asked.

"It'll record you fine, go on," she said impatiently.

"Very well. Okay, it appears that Aggregosh died while having intercourse, indicated by the position of the body and the rut marks of the rear hooves into the dirt. This is further probable given that he has been castrated… for the record, that sound was Danielle voiding her breakfast."

I walked around the body, looking at the dirt. "Is that still recording? Good. The blood saturation in the dirt puts time of death at about seven or eight hours ago. There are recent hoof prints, but only of his, clearly attributed to trotting marks… I can't find any other hoof prints, especially not any small enough to belong to a centaur… female…"

"…M*arling,*" Danielle groaned.

"Marling. No sign, no hair except for the strands from Aggregosh… it would appear that whatever was involved in this was lighter in weight than a centaur and able to avoid disturbing the earth…." I crouched down and peered closely. "There is localised bleeding, extending approximately one metre away from the point of castration. I would have expected more spray from such arterial damage, which leads me to expect that this was a fast action that did not allow the deceased to struggle. Furthermore, the deceased seems to have been caught by surprise… what else… the penile shaft has not been cleanly cut, which has left a ragged" – a groan from Danielle – "edge."

I borrowed the iPad from Danielle and took some pictures of the actual scene using a fifty pence piece from my pocket to give an approximation of size. There was something about the castration that played on my mind... well, more so than castration plays on any man's mind. But this was something other than deep, instinctual, knee touching panic. I pushed the record button again. "The testicles have remained untouched."

Moving away from the body, I did a circle of the tepee's interior. The walls were bare for a space taller than me and then were decorated with trophies and emblems. Most of them were stained with blood, occasionally involving dismembered body parts. The central pole of the tent at around the same height was tightly wound with thick leathery rope, darkened almost black.

"What is that for?" Danielle asked, one arm folded across her body while the other held a hand in front of her mouth.

"Feeling better?"

"Emptier," she said. "I think I've contaminated the scene."

"Well, nobody's perfect," I said.

"So what is that leather for?" she persisted again. I think she was concentrating on something elevated to avoid looking at the dead body.

"It's a makiwara," I said. "A punch board. He would have spent hours hitting it with his fists for training."

"Are we done yet?" she asked.

"Why don't you go wait outside for a second," I suggested. "I have one more thing I need to have a look at."

She didn't argue and a second later I was alone in the tent. I turned off the iPad, put a hand in my pocket and stood back and let the scene take me. This was the home and the training room for a warrior. The earth was packed hard as rock by hoof beats circling that central pole, striking it again and again. I strolled over to the body again and with some effort lifted one of his hands and looked at the back of it. The hands themselves were more leathery than a catcher's mitt but the knuckles were red raw. He had been training the night before – only hours earlier.

No sign of a struggle, the voice in my head said. *A quick, unexpected death that terrified him.*

Castration is terrifying, I reminded myself.

Something else was bugging me though – something playing in the back of my mind and tickling my brain.

I cleared my head, relaxed my eyes and swept my gaze around the interior, passing it gently over the scene until it finally fell upon something.

There were three holes in the dirt, near the tent wall, too close to the tent leather and completely out of place. Two intersecting lines in the dirt about the size of a placemat, orientated so that the one line was directly in line with the corpse.

Outside, Danielle was leaning against the tepee's side, demurely standing with her face in one hand. She was as pale as ivory.

Gregore was approaching. "Are you concluded?" he asked. "Who shall we declare war upon?"

I shook my head. "Nobody yet Gregore," I said. "I need to go through the evidence and I will let you know my findings as soon as I have a confirmed result. You do not want to attack the wrong people."

"We do not attack the innocent," he snarled, which made me think they had been accused of that before.

"I'll be in touch," I said. "Before we go, have you found the penis yet?"

Gregore stamped the ground, "No... not yet."

I nodded. "If it turns up, let me know. Also, was anything removed from the scene?"

"Of course not," he said.

"Even when he was discovered?"

"Nothing was removed, we saw him and we contacted the embassy."

He was getting angry but I did not think he was lying. I helped Danielle to stand up and we made the long walk back to the taxi.

4

Prior to my next meeting I stopped at the office and had a shower and dressed in a fresh suit. When I came out of the bathroom Danielle was standing at my desk with her finger on the iPad. Without looking up she said, "I have taken the liberty of taking your suit to the incinerator, the smell was quite offensive."

"We have an incinerator?" I asked.

"Yes, downstairs," she said, adding quickly, "We're late for your next appointment."

"Remind me."

"The Sisters Havelock," she said.

In short, the Sisters Havelock is a brothel, located in a residential area known locally as the Golden Triangle, which is a wedge-shaped neighbourhood with the thin end of the houses at the city centre with the other corners spreading outwards between Newmarket Road and Earlham Road. It comprises a cosmopolitan mix of students, professionals and families – the whole area is characterised by terrace housing, pubs and parks that offer small festivals during the summer months, such as the GreenStock Festival in

Heigham Park. Sometimes it is nicknamed the Notting Hill of Norwich, and like everything in the city it hid more than it showed.

For example, a brothel that catered specifically to monsters.

"You know," I said, as the driver turned off Earlham Road into Havelock and slowed as he looked for the right door number, "considering what I saw this morning I don't know if I'm up for going into a brothel."

"You are there on official work," Danielle said.

"In what capacity?" I enquired. "Ambassador, Crime Scene Investigator or store-front coordinator?"

"Here we go mate," the driver said, coming to a stop.

We climbed out of the car, and standing on the picturesque road together we approached the very bland looking light blue door with the number eight on it. It didn't look like much – the windows on either side of it had drawn curtains, but as many of these houses were student accommodation with the living rooms transformed into additional bedrooms, this could easily have been a matter of privacy for the occupant and unlikely to draw suspicion. The walls were freshly painted, the small rectangular strip of garden at the front was well kept, despite the cold weather, and there was an element of this property being looked after.

"You're speaking with Mrs Jacqueline Cushion," Danielle said at my side as she knocked on the door with a knuckle.

"I used to live on this road," I said conversationally. "When I first came to the country. It seemed shorter then."

"Strange," Danielle commented. "People usually remember things being longer as they get older."

I was about to reply when the door was opened and a wave of coconut oil perfume washed over us; paradoxically, such a pleasant smell came from the Doorman who had opened the door for us.

A mountain gorilla crammed into a black suit would have seemed more approachable than this character. His shoulders were wider than the width of the doorway; his face was cast in shadow because the light from outside only made it up to his chin, which in itself could have been used to chop wood. It was turning into a morning of giant people.

"Hello," he said.

His voice had the booming quality associated with metal working machinery, and Danielle hiccuped nervously. "We're... um... here to see..."

I almost laughed. I cleared my throat and said, "Could you let Mrs Cushion know that The Ambassador has arrived."

The Doorman didn't move, and his silence lasted for *just* too long before he said, "She is expecting you. Please come in."

He stepped aside and we squeezed past him into a corridor with a wooden slatted floor and walls painted in dark blue with very white coving.

On the left the door was open and led into a very comfortable and above all clean waiting room. We were greeted by a tall woman in a figure hugging white dress.

"Ah! Mr Ambassador," she said with a sparkling smile. "So good to meet you, my name is..."

She gave me her name, but it required some complicated tricks with the tongue and cheek that made my eyes widen. She then said, "My friends call me Lucy."

"Hi Lucy," I said. "Nice to meet you, this is Danielle, my handler."

Danielle and Lucy shook hands and then the taller lady in white put her hands together and said, "I will fetch Jacqueline immediately, she is looking forward to speaking with you."

Lucy left and Danielle turned on me. "What is that standing at the door?"

"A Doorman," I said. "You don't know?"

"I don't frequent these kinds of places," she said, but there was no venom in her tone. I thought she was blushing.

Jacqueline flowed into the room a moment later. Unlike Lucy, she was not the typical beauty. Instead she was mostly round, with a big bum and a gargantuan chest wrapped up in a green dress with just enough flowing bits to make her look graceful. Her hair was just as big as her body, a vast blast of brown and blond curls. All of this was dwarfed the moment you saw her wide, happy and perfectly gorgeous smile.

"Donnie, Danielle," she cried, slipping easily into a first name basis with both of us and embracing us in turn with a full on and very breasty hug.

Mrs Cushion, what a perfect name.

Jacqueline insisted on showing us around before settling down for lunch. She was very proud of what she had been able to create in her home. The official schematics of the house were of an upstairs and downstairs two bedroom house, but, beyond the doors there were seventeen rooms, four bath areas and a very large kitchen.

"At any time we are entertaining royalty and working class alike," she said, "of all kinds of species, even some in-the-know humans. They all come to my little place of business to satisfy their urges and their tastes. It's better that it's done in a controlled environment by people who care rather than out on the street where things get... dicey."

The working girls who wandered the corridors were all beautiful and clothed, if revealingly. None of them were human. "Are they all daughters of Lilith?" I asked when we were shown into the kitchen, where the centre island was straining under a smorgasbord of fruits and cheeses.

Jacqueline beamed a radiant smile. "Oh you have a good eye, but I should have expected it. You are very well acquainted with Madam Thankeron as I understand?"

Danielle's head turned so sharply her fringe swung from one side of her head to the other.

"Yes," I said, not looking at her. "We have a history."

Jacqueline seemed happy with this. "The Daughters of Lilith are best suited for this role… they are talented, well versed and above all physically inclined to it."

We enjoyed lunch, washing it down with some exotic fruit punch. Jacqueline explained all the elements to us; the health and safety, the insurances and especially the security.

"Wraith Security," she said with an easy shrug that hid the severity of her choice. "Best that money can buy and very effective."

Both Danielle and myself cast a ginger eye around the interior of the house. Danielle seemed satisfied and closed down her iPad in such a manner as to say that business was concluded. Jacqueline looked momentarily confused, before I rallied to explain –

"Oh, I'm just a rubber stamp my dear," I said through a smile. "But I do have a question I wanted to ask."

"Shoot."

"Do you allow access for halfies?"

The brothel owner's expression landed with a thud and her tone was almost threatening. "My girls are very valuable."

"I believe there are many halfies who have money," I speculated.

"I meant for me," Jacqueline said, adding rather directly, "Should I have elaborated further about health and safety? I'm not putting my girls into jeopardy."

"Do you mean that a halfie would pose a threat to their health?"

"Not all halfies," Jacqueline relented. "But... some..."

I took my time with the next question, ignoring the waves of cold that were radiating off of Danielle. I finished the remainder of my juice. "Do you have coffee by any chance?"

Jacqueline waved a hand and a girl detached herself from the wall and went to work brewing me some. While the water boiled I put a finger onto the table and traced the fine grain of it with a fingertip. "Mrs Cushion, you are a brothel owner so I know that you are discrete, but also probably prefer people being direct with their desires. Would you deny someone of my position his desires?"

Next to me Danielle sighed. Jacqueline's expression, if possible, dropped several other levels.

"No," she said.

"Very good," I said. "Your business is very pleasing and, above all, discrete. I appreciate this. But if I were a centaur where would I go for my pleasure?"

"*Not here.*"

I was calm. "From your tone I imagine that they have approached you before?"

She regained her composure. Like the sun breaching the line of the horizon her expression returned to the delightful business owner she had been moments before. It lacked some of its shine now that I knew it was genuinely skin deep. We waited until the coffee was served on a tray in cosmopolitan glasses. We all took up our coffees and Jacqueline asked her girl to leave the kitchen and close the door behind her.

When alone, Jacqueline told us, "We often have to turn away halfies, not just horses but wolves, bulls and rhinos. The last time though was earlier this year. A gang of them came here asking to be permitted. I want it known that we were very civil, but the centaurs are too big to come inside the house, or inside one of my girls for that matter. They asked if they could hire some of the girls out for an evening but even in these enlightened times, street walking is illegal. So I declined their offer and their money."

"Did you suggest an alternative venue?" I asked. The coffee was strong, very strong. I tasted it in my bone marrow.

"Oh I didn't have to!" she exclaimed. "They left by themselves."

"That sounds unlikely," Danielle said.

"Wraith Security," I said in passing. "It would make the front of this building as solid as a mountain."

"Quite right," Jacqueline agreed. "But my Doorman was still about to get involved because we didn't want them loitering at the front of our building and they were scaring away business. But just as things started to get heated a woman walked by and suggested another venue."

"A woman?"

"She looked like a human woman," Jacqueline said. "Which... you know?... I found weird because she seemed to notice that they were halfies and it didn't even scare her. It was as if she had been looking for business. She looked at me then spoke to the gang of horses and said, 'This place is a little soft for your liking anyway – you want a place where the girls will push back.'"

Danielle spluttered her coffee.

"They went away then?" I pressed, absently handing Danielle a napkin.

"Sure did," Jacqueline said. "Haven't had any enquiries or problems from their like at all since then."

"Do you have any idea where this place is?"

"No idea," Jacqueline said. "Frankly they're not my competition if they're taking that kind of clientele. In fact they are actually helping my business so I didn't see a need to interfere."

"Is it really a human brothel?" Danielle asked.

"Don't be silly my girl," Jacqueline said. "Have you ever seen a centaur's penis?"

On our way out I gave Jacqueline my number and said, "If you hear any more news about centaurs please let me know."

She shrugged. "I don't take much interest in it, but if that is your wish I will see what I can find."

"No, no," I said. "Only if you hear something. Thank you for your time."

In the taxi Danielle waited until we had turned the corner before turning to me and saying, "You could be smarter than you look."

I, however, wasn't smart enough to know how to take that so I let her find a suitable response in my silence.

5

The third meeting was conducted and settled so quickly and surreptitiously that it barely registered on the calendar. The taxi stopped outside my flat and Danielle asked, "I'll be in the office at 7AM tomorrow if you want?"

"I have gym first thing, but I'll be there as soon as I can," I promised. I got out of the taxi and watched it rejoin the traffic. I walked down the dumpster lined alleyway that led to the front door of my building, ignoring the dubious puddles in the corners and not questioning the strange smells that were redolent from the dumpsters. I emptied my mailbox, let myself in and walked up the wide staircase to the first floor to Number 8. The eight decoration itself was slightly faded on one side so it looked like a stunted, reverse three, but as the apartment took up the whole of the floor it was of little concern.

Inside, I put on some music, poured myself a tall drink to counteract the twitchy effects of the coffee I had drunk at the whorehouse and all but collapsed in my Chesterfield, which was positioned to allow me to stare at the wide brick wall that covered the entire western half of my flat.

Someone once remarked that I am specific about what I allow to distract me. The brick wall was a fine example. You see, the apartment never used to have a big brick wall; instead it was a detail that appeared one day, as if it had just pushed its way out of the plaster wall like ice blocks rising out of cream. It didn't bother me. It didn't hurt me, but it did fascinate me. It looked stylish and the fact that it should have been impossible was easily filed in a mental catalogue labelled 'Should Be Impossible' that was at this time one of the thickest files in my mind.

It was a useful wall to stare at.

Staring at something that you know is impossible that is nevertheless there helps put things into perspective and opens up the mind marvellously.

After exactly twenty minutes I took up my phone and sent a text to Danielle.

NOTE FOR TOMORROW. I THINK WE NEED TO CHANGE MY TITLE. MR AMBASSADOR ISN'T WORKING. I LIKE PRIVATE EYE.

My phone buzzed a moment later with a text.

WILL LOOK INTO IT. IT'S PRIVATE I, AS IN PI, AS IN PRIVATE INVESTIGATOR.

I put my phone down and returned to watching the brick wall.

A moment later my phone buzzed again. *AND YOU ARE NOT A PI.*

A person said, "The television is behind you, you know?"

"This is more interesting," I replied.

An awkward silence precipitated. One that lasted a long time and was detailed only by the sound of traffic on the busy road outside and the uncertain shuffling of a person not knowing what to do. I twisted around in the Chesterfield and saw my unexpected guest standing in the kitchenette looking abashed.

"What's wrong?" I asked.

"I expected you to jump," she admitted.

"Why would I do that?"

"I appeared unexpectedly," she explained, "I was very careful in my approach, fastidious in my manner of concealment and you could not have expected my arrival."

"Everything really starts by the fifth chapter," I answered, getting comfortable again and returning to staring at the bricks. I could have sworn the brick I'd been watching had moved. "Who are you anyway? What do you want?"

"My name is Wandilyn," she said. "I am the daughter of Jason Marcadius."

"I know that name," I said. "He is The Old Man Forgetful?"

"Quite correct," she said.

"I never forgot him," I pointed out with a smirk.

"Which is why I have come to you. I understand that you are an investigator?"

I glanced at my phone. News couldn't travel that fast.

"Not officially," I said. "I was an Ambassador up until a moment ago."

"Oh sir, you have to be though!" Miss Wandilyn cried, approaching and falling to her knees with such speed that on reflex I stood. She clung to the arm of my chair. "You are the only man who remembers my father, the only person who can find his killer!"

"Forgive me," I said, "but this is all a bit sudden. I'm already in the middle of something and my time is..."

"Valuable, I know!" she cried, tears brimming in her eyes. "But only you can help me, surely you must be able to help?"

I spread my arms beseechingly. "How can I help when I don't even know what the problem is? Will you sit? And please, or a start, calm the fuck down."

The woman perched on the double seater sofa and clung one of the throw cushions to her chest while I went to the cabinet and poured more drink into my glass.

"Would you like some rum?" I asked.

"Vodka," she said. "If you have it?"

As I poured the drinks and added ice I kept my back to her and did my best to remember what she looked like, but discovered I couldn't. Did she have auburn hair like the first fallen leaves of autumn or blonde hair like the colour of corn? Were her eyes emerald gems or blue sapphires? Was she white or was she black? Asian? Or a creamy mixture?

Returning and handing her the drink I turned my chair away from the wall to face her. She said, "It is as my father said, you cannot remember?"

"I remember your existence," I said. "I remember that you are a woman of medium height, that you are attractive and look healthy and even athletic, but when you leave I won't be able to remember any specific descriptions of you.

It is like my mind doesn't want to hold the information."

"What can you remember of my father?" she asked.

"Tall man," I said. "Lanky like a rake but strong. Deceptively so, it was like his muscles were made out of coat hangers. Quick like a freak too. I want to say that he had dark hair? Slicked back like a gentleman from the 1950s, but I am probably wrong. Mostly I remember that he made unbelievably good coffee and was a great cook. And he laughed from his stomach. You say that he is dead though?"

She nodded sadly, her eyes staring at the carpet. "Killed."

"I'm sorry to hear that," I said. "Forgive me asking but I assume you suspect there was foul play?"

"Why else would I come to a private investigator?" she asked.

"Kind of my point," I said, hiding the smile at the part where she referred to me as a private investigator; I liked the term. "May I ask what happened?"

She sniffed and finished her vodka with a single swig. I refilled her glass for her and returned to my seat, leaning forward attentively.

"I came home last night and found him," she said, choking back a sob. "He was in the bedroom, on the bed, dead."

"Was it obvious how he died?"

"Oh my God, what a question!"

"I thought it was a good question," I said, then realising she had not been complimenting me, rallied with some tact and assured her. "It is relevant. I'm sure."

"Well, yes then. I could tell how he had died," she said. "His cock was missing."

6.

Miss Wandilyn and I spoke well into the night before she left. Afterwards I stood at the window staring at my reflection in the glass and wondering with a fairly addled brain if perhaps it would have been more professional if I hadn't drunk all that rum and then suggested she stay over.

As it was, it didn't matter. In terms of who she could ask for help she didn't have a choice. I was the only man who was able to remember her father at all and able to retain a somewhat clear recollection of her. Also, it seemed to be the same killer who had taken down the gargantuan Aggregosh who killed her father. The evening had not ended on a brilliant note: at the door she had agreed to come to the office the morning and called me a pig. I turned to go to bed and promptly fell over.

Danielle looked up at me sideways when I walked into the office, and in response to this scathing expression I checked my watch. "I am on time."

"You asked her to stay the night?" my personal assistant growled.

"Wow, it does travel fast after all," I said. "How did you know?"

"Whispers," she said.

Ah yes, the Whispers: The otherwise annoying Otherwise and Late communication network of ethereal communication.

"I was drunk," I defended weakly. "Is she here?"

"Yes," Miss Wandilyn said directly behind me, making me jump.

"You did that on purpose!" I yelped.

"You deserved it," she said, crossing her arms and appraising me. "You look remarkably chipper for a man who drank a bottle of Kraken by himself."

I gave her my best grin, "As do you for someone who's just lost their father."

"Oh!" she exclaimed.

I looked down at Danielle, who looked about to stab me with her pen. Knowing that I had passed the point of any salvation with both of these women I decided to go for broke.

"I'll have my coffee in the office Danielle," I sad blankly, then to Miss Wandilyn I said, "Would you care to join me in there where we can discuss the case?"

"You're not a PI!" Danielle snarled as she walked to the kitchenette.

I offered Miss Wandilyn a seat before walking around my desk to my own chair and sitting down. I allowed myself a moment to ponder my line of questioning.

"Your desk is very tidy," she said, interrupting my train of thought.

"I like to keep a clean desk," I said. "Helps me keep a clear mind. No distractions and all that."

"Or Danielle just doesn't like mess," she countered.

I smiled and rocked gently in my chair. "I would say that this is a delicate case but I happen to know that it will not be. Your family line is so forgettable even the Otherwise, Late and most of the Lost have trouble recalling you."

"For those who can remember him, my father was a great man," Wandilyn said stonely. "Cherished."

"I considered him my friend," I acknowledged.

"He considered you to be a disreputable gent with an out of control libido," she told me.

"It's what he liked about me," I said.

Danielle brought in the coffee, handing Miss Wandilyn hers and all but throwing mine at me. I waited for her to leave before wiping my tie with a handkerchief and saying, "The issue is that your father made many enemies, given his career."

"Which one?" she asked, with keenly honed innocence.

"Good point. Your father was useful in many different circumstances. Thief, assassin, spy… which one do you think he was killed for?"

"None of those," she said. "I do not believe he was murdered for anything that he had done."

I had to agree with the woman, it was unlikely that the ghost that was Jason Marcadius would have been killed for revenge. He was an Old Man Forgetful, and his targets had been very carefully chosen. I was certain that none of them could remember. He was a man who could be traced only by what was not there.

"If we start at the obvious suspects," I suggested. "What of his employers? They may have reason to want him removed after he had outlived his usefulness."

"It is terribly tragic but none of his employers are alive anymore," she said.

I let the statement hang in the air for a little while before continuing.

"Did your father ever have any dealings with centaurs?"

She wrinkled her nose. "No, of course not."

"Are you certain?"

"Yes," she said. "He never had any cause to, and do you remember how he used to dress?"

I had the impression that I did remember exactly how pressed and perfect his clothes were. A trouser crease like the folded edge of a birthday card, ties of silk and shoes so polished they shone. An absolute gentleman in every sense of the word, but I couldn't hold onto the details for long and it did leave me with a sombre feeling – Jason Marcadius was gone.

"You suddenly look very sad," she commented.

"I liked your dad," I said. "He was a kind man. A criminal through and through, but he was one of the most honourable and noble men I've ever known. I miss him already."

"Tell me, honestly," she said. "Do you think you can find his killer and bring them to justice?"

"What kind of justice are we talking about?" I asked.

She sighed, as if finding it tiresome to have to even discuss such matters. "Ambassador or private investigator, everyone knows your history. Late, Lost or Otherwise know where you were schooled."

"How do you think I met your father?"

"He told me about how you two met," she said. "I feel that he would rejoice in the idea that you have taken on this contract. You know how he felt about debts."

"I am well aware that I owe your father," I said, perhaps too severely. "But I won't kill anyone for you."

"Fine," she said, opening up her purse and withdrawing a very heavy looking envelope. "I will be satisfied with just their name. I will pay you for as much."

The envelope thumped on the desk just as she rose from her chair. "I will contact you in forty-eight hours to see what you have discovered. Good day to you detective."

She let herself out and I sat staring at the envelope long after she had left. The contents of it had spilled out, revealing several bricks of fifty pound notes.

I opened the centre drawer of my desk and swept the envelope and its bricks into it. Ramming the drawer shut, I called to Danielle, "Are you still my personal assistant if I'm no longer the Ambassador?"

"You are *not* a private investigator," she replied from the other room. "However, I am assigned to you whether you are the Ambassador or not."

I smiled. "Very good, what meetings do I have today?"

"None," she said.

"Do you remember Miss Wandilyn?" I asked as I went to her desk.

"Who?" she asked, her eyebrows knitting above her nose.

"Never mind," I said. "Call us a taxi will you? We're going to the centaur's camp, I need to find out where this brothel of theirs is."

7.

Gregore was not at the camp when we arrived. He and a hunting party had gone out to hunt winchikari, or so said the elderly centaur who was busy reducing a very large animal into steaks. The species of the beast was impossible to identify as its hide had already been removed and was currently drying on a scaffold. The elderly centaur female had white hair that was tied back and plaited into a long tail that hung off her back. She wore the straps and vestments of a warrior but moved in an awkward shamble due to a crooked leg. I had been under the impression that the centaurs did not retain their lame, yet the way she handled a knife as she removed great big slabs of meat from the slain beast answered the question of how she could still be alive.

"What is a winchikari?" I asked Danielle, looking down at my Wellington boots to avoid the marling's gaze.

"Nightmare demon," Danielle said with a shudder. "Horrible creatures, not from this plane."

"Oh, like vampires?" I asked.

"Not so simply," Danielle said.

"The little pixie is right," the marling said, bringing down her knife and shearing through half a foot of meat as if it were foam. "They are wraiths that feed off terror and fear. Not for sustenance, but out of enjoyment."

"They are corporeal?"

"Yes," the centaur said. "Of course you have to bring down the adults."

"Is that when they become corporeal?"

The marling gave me a severe look. "No, because you do not hunt younglings of any creature."

The full stop hit the end of her sentence like an arrow. She returned to de-meating the corpse next to her stall but I didn't leave; finally she relented and looked away from the meat. "What?"

"Do you know when Gregore will return?" I enquired.

"Could be days," she answered. "Who knows?"

Danielle started to depart but I caught her arm and held her still. To the marling I said, "I would suspect you would know though. I'm sorry but I was very rude and I didn't ask your name."

"I am a cripple," the marling answered bitterly. "I have no name."

"What do your friends call you?"

"No name, no friends," she said, trotting awkwardly to the ribcage, where each rib was the thickness of a kayak. She dug her fingers into a curtain slab of meat and with a grunt tore it from the bone as if it were barely attached. She returned to her table and swatted away some flies.

"You are still here?" she gruffed.

"I am sorry, but I like to know the names of people I speak with," I said. "If I am going to be in debt with someone it is easier to keep a tally if you have a name."

"Debt?" She said the word sharply, but there was interest there.

"You are old and crippled," I said. "Which means you watch. You pay attention I'm sure, as all the old do."

She nodded.

"I am investigating the assassination of Aggregosh," I said. "I need to know the name of a brothel in the city that the centaur menfolk visit."

She spat between two of her meat tables. "Damned fools."

"Is it foolish to pay for the services of professionals?"

"The menfolk have womenfolk," the marling said.

Ah, I thought. I had noticed that the marling's hindleg was the one that was crippled; centaurs were mounters. She would be unable to hold the weight of a male.

"This debt," she said. "Would it be between you and me?"

I nodded.

She looked me up and down, keeping in mind that she was a good five feet taller than I, and seemed to decide something. She said, "I will help you but I will hold you to the debt."

Next to me Danielle snorted.

"What would you ask of me?" I asked, my voice cracking.

"I am often left here alone," she said. "I have no name and so nobody speaks with me. I am useful and so I am tolerated, I am dangerous so I am left alone. But I cannot hunt and because I am lame, I cannot rut. You will come to me next time I am left here alone."

The question, 'What is the worst that could happen?', passed through my mind, and was quickly followed by a panicked list.

"Of course," I said.

She nodded, satisfied. "My name is Mary."

I put on my shoes and tossed the muddied wellies into the trunk of the taxi and sneered at Danielle's laughter.

When I joined her in the backseat even the taxi driver was spluttering.

"Shut up both of you," I said.

"If it's any help sir," the driver said from the front. "We can stop off at the camping store and get you a sleeping bag!"

"That's vile," I said. "Can you take us to this address?"

I gave him a slip of paper from my notebook and he took it and laughed. "Getting some first-hand experience are you?"

"You know this place?"

"I've never been there but I know the address. Sometimes our firm is called to pick up girls who have to go get stitched up, if you know what I mean?"

I did and what he said stopped Danielle from laughing so abruptly he brought about a very uncomfortable silence inside the cab. The driver turned the ignition on and got off the curb and drove in silence for an hour before Danielle's phone rang.

Answering, she didn't say anything and just listened in silence for over a minute, her face becoming harder and angrier with each passing second. It ended with her saying simply "I'll let him know," and hanging up.

"Can I assume 'him' is me?" I enquired.

"It was Norwich City Council," she said. "It is regarding your title as Ambassador."

"Go on,"

"They say that Private Investigator indicates that you are self-employed, if this is so they cannot keep you on the payroll."

A moment's panic hit me so hard it was like being electrocuted. Gratefully, she continued;

"They have indicated, however, that they do approve of your new position. They are happy with you playing the role of detective if you feel it is more suited and they will continue to fund you assuming you will take on cases they put your way."

I smiled, but this confounded me on two fronts. Firstly, I had rejoiced in the rebellion of my actions, savoured the thrill of sticking my nose in places it was not welcomed. Secondly, it proved something which had been suggested before, that infuriated me. Like a child allowed to pretend to be whatever it wants as long as he obeys the law of his parents, I was no freer than a pre-schooler.

"You are smiling but you don't seem happy," she observed. "I thought this is what you wanted?"

"I am still an employee," I said.

"You always were," she said, "But you still have your independence."

"Because I decided I didn't want to be called Ambassador anymore?"

"Well, carry on doing this until you get bored with it, then do something else. Become a baker or something?"

What a notion. Even if I did become a baker and spent my days in a shop behind a counter, up to my elbows in flour and wearing a hairnet, the Council would still find a way to get me involved with them.

"Maybe I will," I said.

Then we were hit in the flank by something. It was a thunderous collision to the passenger's side, sharply changing the direction of the front wheels and causing the entire vehicle to flip itself over into a cartwheel. I acted instinctively as Danielle's seat belt failed and she was flung forward. My fingers dug into the fine fabric of her suit jacket, my fingernails bending back against the force of her movement and I wrapped her up in my arms, one arm around her tiny waist and the other hand pressing the back of her head into my shoulder while my own belt dug and cut into my waist.

The driver was not so lucky and he rattled around his cabin like a rag doll before disappearing out the window with a smash of glass scarcely heard in the crashing of the vehicle.

Off the road we went, and down the hill into the moors until finally coming to rest at the foot of the hill, amazingly with all four wheels on the ground.

"Danielle, you're choking me," I wheezed.

Shakily, she unwound her arms from around my neck and said, shivering like a mouse, "What the hell happened?"

"We got hit," I explained, depositing her on the seat beside me and unbuckling the seatbelt.

She looked at the seatbelt she had been using. "I had mine on," she gasped.

"So did the driver," I said. "You got lucky."

"I got lucky because of you," she said. "How did you move so fast?"

I unbuckled myself and tried the door handle but it didn't budge. I climbed out of the window.

"No seriously," Danielle said, following me out. "How did you do that?"

"Luck."

"I don't believe you," she said.

"Well," I said as I helped her to the ground. "Let's not test a working theory right now."

With her hand in mine I led her away from the car, heading back in the direction we had been coming from along the bottom of the hill. The sky had clouded over again to a pencil shade grey that seemed to cover the entire world. The ground was soggy and covered in stubby grass a brownish grey shade. The small hill leading up to the road was the highest point for as far as the eye could see.

After a minute or so I angled up towards the crest of the hill and the road. Keeping low I peeked over the top and scanned the road up and down.

"Nothing's there," Danielle observed happily, then spying my face she asked in a worried tone. "What?"

"Nothing's there," I said.

"Look!" she whispered loudly, pointing. "The driver's there."

She started to get up and I pulled her to the ground. She struggled and I clapped a hand over her mouth and held a finger to my lips, then pointing with two fingers at my eyes I pointed them at where the driver lay.

One word could describe how the driver looked – smeared. His body had remained together, but everything inside had been smeared out in front of him for several metres. I would never be able to think of the word *smeared* again without thinking of the sum of his entrails, in the cold air, steaming and twitching. Unless you've seen how much entrails move when they're still connected you'll never be prepared for that desperate quiver. Meanwhile his arms were moving and his chest was heaving as he struggled to breathe with what remained in his chest cavity.

Danielle struggled against me but I held her firm.

Something on the other side of the road moved. A brief jittery movement, a jerky shift of what I had perceived to be a dark rock on the other side of the road. Another jerk revealed a face that made Danielle freeze in my arms.

Like a chameleon at high speed, moving in a number of unnatural, stop motion jerks, the creature rose from the other side of the hill.

Its face was blackened and distorted, like a burnt and broken pumpkin shell. Two blackened holes represented eyes, a third smaller one represented a nose, and there was the distinct look of an upper mandible but no lower. The creature lacked a jawbone. Instead hanging from it was a black tentacle tongue that whipped around loosely with each jerk. Its arms were long, made up of the same number of joints as a primate's arms but with the forearms being longer than the rest of it, and it walked on the back of its long and flat hands, with disjointed fingers curling upwards towards its wrists. Its shoulders were big and round, covered in useless fine hair that hung off the back of its head to droop over its shoulders. Like its jaw, it lacked lower extremities, its body ending just below its ribcage, visible beneath parchment thin black skin. A backbone with a pelvic crown curled beneath it like a tail.

It hesitated at the side of the road, jerking its head from side to side, erratically shifting its body weight against its two crane-like arms. Deciding that it was safe to proceed, it approached the fallen driver.

Danielle started to shake like a tiny bird but didn't run. If anything it felt like she was trying to get closer to me, as if to hide inside me if she could.

Frustratingly irregular, the creature walked to the driver and leant in close. The driver, alive enough to witness this, started to scream.

It was a scream of a man realising that this was the last thing he would see in this world. The scream of someone who has lost the hope of dying in a warm comfortable bed surrounded by loved ones. It was a haunting scream that cursed the indifference of the universe.

His scream worsened when the next thing happened.

The creature leant its head back with the first graceful movement, and lowered its rib cage towards the driver's face. The ribs snapped open like the legs of a spider and the backbone arched backwards, and with a vicious wet crunch all of it slammed together around the driver's head.

A period of brittle wet sounds followed, each one making Danielle flinch.

The creature was not eating the driver, it was not consuming him – instead it straightened its arms and rose with the driver's body, now head deep in the creature's torso hanging below it. The driver's feet, one still wearing a shoe and the other, shoeless, bent at an awkward angle at the ankle, dangled a foot from the road. His entrails dragged along the tarmac and made me think of my tongue being drawn across sandpaper.

The driver's body began flinching and his arms and legs jerked spasmodically. Whatever the creature was doing to him had not yet finished because the entrails were dropped out of its body, cut off by whatever was now anchored within the driver and left to fall wetly onto the road between its back bent hands.

The body curled up, the knees drawing up to the chest and the arms enveloping them in a hug as if the driver was going foetal. Then the body in one movement opened up again, arms and legs stretching out. The movement was repeated again.

It's flexing, I thought with horror.

The creature turned, and walked, the driver's bent legs swaying gently beneath it, along the trail of wreckage that led to the torn up turf on the side of road where the car had left it.

As it did I found Danielle's hand and I pushed us away from the hillside.

Keeping an eye on the creature I timed it just right as it started down the hill towards the broken car. I took Danielle and pulled her up onto the road.

"Won't it see us up here?"

"It's going to see us anywhere we go," I said. "There is nowhere to hide, but the road is easier to run on than down in the moors."

"We're heading away from the city though," she whispered.

"Oh, that's a good point."

"And it's getting dark," she whined.

"Hmm," I said.

Behind us there was a shriek. High pitched and wet, a disturbingly unnatural sound, and while the creature didn't come fully into sight we could see its sharp shoulders jutting and jogging as it ran up at us.

Shoving Danielle behind me I stood to face the creature as it approached and with ludicrous bravado I raised my fists.

"You are such an idiot," Danielle whimpered behind me.

"Oh good," I said as the creature climbed onto the road. "It's *armed.*"

Clutched in its newly acquired hands the monster held torn off pieces of metal from the taxi. Crude, but highly effective weaponry.

"You can't be serious," Danielle gasped as she saw me change my stance.

"Do you have your iPad?" I asked.

"It was broken so I left it," she said.

"Good, don't stop at the taxi then," I said. "Start running to the city as soon as you see my signal."

"What signal?" she asked.

"Something incredibly idiotic," I said.

The creature hesitated though. It lingered where it had been found, rocking from side to side. It seemed to be considering something, then, it started moving away from us, towards the other side of the road where it had been hiding previously. As it did this I found Danielle's hand and led her forward so that as the creature descended down the hill, still watching us, we passed it.

Gradually the creature dropped out of sight, its baleful gaze scorching the tufts of grass that passed in front of it.

After long minutes of walking, gingerly observing the sides of the road, expecting at any minute for the thing to burst out at us, Danielle asked the obvious question.

"What did you do?"

"Nothing," I admitted.

"It looked like you scared it off," she said, a touch of admiration in her voice.

"I can be very scary when I want to be," I said.

"Maybe it was full," she considered.

That could be it, I thought, but I wasn't convinced.

8.

The moors gave way to drier land and the ground on either side of the road became gradually higher and presented fewer places to hide. Night came, falling like a shutter over the land but the moon, bright and bold, pierced the thin layer of clouds, presenting us with more than enough light to walk with.

"Should we stop and make a fire?" Danielle asked.

"If you want to go looking for firewood you're welcome to," I said. "But I'd rather not."

She curled her arms around my arm a bit tighter.

"Are you afraid?" I asked.

"Of course," she said. "Aren't you?"

"I don't know," I answered. "Probably. But I'm waiting for something."

"For what?"

"A sign," I said.

We continued in silence, Danielle still clinging to my arm in the dark, the road in front of us a slightly less dark strip in an otherwise black soup.

The moonlight was good, but lazy when it came to getting into some of the darker shadows.

"What was your signal going to be?" she asked. "The one you said was going to be idiotic?"

"I was going to fight that thing," I told her.

"Did you think you could win?"

"I assumed that I would find a way."

"I don't know if that's arrogance or determination," she said.

"Determination," I said. "You need to be a smart man to be arrogant. Ah, here we are."

"Where?" she asked.

"The sign."

The sign was another road, that cut the road we were on at a perfect ninety degree angle, forming an absolutely perfect cross; this mathematical precision was the sign, for there were no other road signs.

Danielle didn't understand but I took her hands from my arm and asked, "Do you remember us going past a crossroads?"

"No," she said.

"Precisely," I said, looking around.

"What are you searching for?"

"Somewhere to sit down," I said. "My eyes aren't so hot in this gloom, can you see anywhere?"

She pointed to the nearest corner, "There is a stump there."

"Can you tell what wood it is?"

"Hickory," she said. "Which is strange, you don't get hickory in these parts."

I told her to stay where she was and went to the stump. I walked around it once and caught her watching me with interest; she spread her arms questioningly and I held out a hand begging for her patience and sat down on the stump.

From the centre of the crossroad someone started to clap. I glanced over to where Danielle had been standing to find that she wasn't there. I looked over at the new arrival and spied a figure sitting in a chair of carved wood and leather. The figure had one leg crossed over the other and was dressed in a very fine tuxedo with a bow tie. His shoes were so polished the moonlight glinted off them but he didn't have a face, or much of a head. Instead there was a great geyser of perpetual smoke, in which I had the impression of something with horns and eyes that were so dark and empty that they sucked the vapours into them.

"Well done Mr Rust," the figure said.

"Don't get too excited," I told the newcomer. "Got a bit of the story left to get through so you can't be too dramatic."

The figure said nothing for a moment. I had the impression he was smiling. "Do you who I am?"

"The devil?"

"One of them at least," he laughed, his voice booming across the night. "I figured that you were in need of some help. I saw an opportunity to make a deal."

I nodded.

"But you know that I know who you are."

"Which title are your referring to?" I asked.

"Ambassador, Detective..." he said the words as if tasting them. "I think I prefer your other title more."

"My other title?"

The problem with Debt Devils is that they know everything about you. If the sum of all your deeds, sins and indiscretions were written down, they would have the transcripts ready to read. They were tapped into the fabric of things and they only ever appeared when they knew they could gain something from it.

"We will come to that later I am sure," the devil said to me. "But for now, I am willing to speak with you with whichever title you choose. Titles mean little to me, after all. I have been taking notes. But to follow what you said to me, I am surprised that you came to me so soon in the story."

"We are being hunted by a monster," I said.

"You are a man who is often hunted by monsters," the devil said. "Aside from this one following you what difference should it make?"

I shrugged.

"Fair enough."

"I want to get back to the city safely as I have a case to solve," I explained.

"You are taking this new title seriously aren't you?"

"I think it is important that I do," I said. "And a man must take his hobbies seriously."

The devil chuckled. "You wish me to get you home safely?"

"If I were to make a deal," I said, "it would be for my friend Danielle's and my total safety. We

78

would both need to be returned home alive and well."

"Sounds simple enough," the devil said. "And in return?"

"I would suspect that you already have a trade in mind," I said. "Let's cut to the chase sir, this was meant to be a short chapter."

The devil seemed perturbed for just a second, then settled back into its chair. It spread its hands to indicate the four different routes. "But isn't this such a good time for me to enter in? Like these roads, the story could go in any direction from here... are you to be a hero or a villain, a martyr or a coward?"

I sighed and stood. "We have walked a long time and I think this was a mistake. We'll take our chances with the monster."

"Wait, Mister Detective," the devil said, leaning forward. "You are correct, I do have a trade in mind and of course I will be able to help you."

"What is your suggested trade?"

"I require only your services."

I sat down again. "I beg your pardon?"

The devil leant an arm on his knee. "Your services Mister Detective," he repeated. "The killer you are seeking... I would require her."

"Her?" I said.

The devil removed a small notebook from his inner jacket pocket and paged through it – he made an annoyed sound and muttered to himself. "These are usually more accurate. It says here that you should have known who the killer was by now."

I held my hands to my side. "You might as well tell me now," I said.

He objected, waving a finger at me as he put the notebook back into his pocket. "No no no, it doesn't work like that. This is a deal, I can get you back to the city and you give me the soul of the murderer, whoever or whatever *it* may be, and if you forfeit I get your rope."

"My rope?" I said. "I'm sorry sir, but you've lost me. Why do you want my rope?"

The devil's fingers drummed on the armrest of his chair for a second then with a sigh he consulted his notebook again, pointing a finger at a page. "You are supposed to know this!"

I shrugged. "Know what? What's a rope got to do with anything?"

The devil put a hand into the smoking geyser that was his head, massaging temples I imagined that I couldn't see. "This is all so frustrating. Just agree to the deal and I'll get you home safe and sound."

From the inky blackness beyond the crossroads came a gargled scream that carried across the land. I looked behind me into the night. "Fine," I said.

Looking back suddenly the devil was right in front of me. An unexpected coolness radiated off his body and instead of the traditional sulphur he smelt like lavender. I mentioned it.

"We like to move with the times," he said, holding out a hand. "Shake it and the deal is made."

I shook his hand.

The devil smiled a ragged tear behind the smoke and stepped back, then raised his long, ivory fingers to his lips and whistled loudly. Headlights appeared in the distance and soon became a black stretch limousine. It pulled up next to us and the rear door sprung open revealing Danielle sitting inside, looking furious.

"My driver caught her and had to bring her back," the devil said. "He says she was running towards the city."

"She was doing what I told her," I said, then turning back to the devil I tried to reason with him. "It would be so much easier if you just told me what you know about the killer."

He smiled and slipped an envelope into my jacket pocket. "I am afraid it doesn't work like that. This way I have leverage and a guarantee and that's exactly what my kind of devil likes." He patted my breast pocket. "This is to be presented to our murderer."

"What is it?"

"An invitation to my home of course," he said, holding the door for me.

He closed the door for me and the limousine glided off smoothly. Danielle punched me hard in the arm.

"Ouch!" I yelped. "What the hell was that for?"

"For being an utter prat," she snarled, "You just made a deal with the devil at a crossroads!"

"I knew it was coming," I said. "So I made the best of the situation as I could."

"You knew it was coming?"

"My seatbelt didn't fail," I explained. "The luck of the devil usually means you're getting a deal whether you like it or not."

"So the monster was sent by the devil?"

"One of them."

"What? There are more monsters?"

"No," I said. "There are more devils. In total there are seven Debt Devils and that was one of them."

"It sounds like you have experience dealing with these devils – have you made a deal in the past?"

I leant into the extravagantly comfortable limousine seat and stretched out my legs. "You know, I think I might have done."

9.

As agreed the limousine delivered us safely to my flat. I insisted that Danielle take the spare room and while she had a shower I made up the bed for her. Once she was done I took a long shower, trying to wash away the pain from the thousand individual aches. Nothing had been broken in the crash but the bruises went right down to the bone.

Afterwards I pulled on a pair of chinos and a loose linen shirt and went through to the living room where Danielle was standing staring at the brick wall.

"Did you put this in here?" she asked.

"No," I said. "It appeared by itself. Can I get you a drink?"

"It doesn't bother you that your flat is changing around you?"

"It might do," I acknowledged. "But it's on a sliding scale and architecture has slid quite a way down. Would you like a coffee?"

She was wearing the tracksuit I had given her – it was too small for me but even with the arms and legs rolled up completely she was swimming in it. She said no to the coffee. "I have an early rise in the morning," she said. "I need to get the backup to my iPad. Aren't you tired?"

"I'll stay up and stare at the wall for a bit," I said. "I'll see you in the morning."

"Don't be late," she said.

"I'll keep trying," I replied.

As she walked past she asked, "Did this room used to belong to Nikita? The owner of the coffee shop?"

"Yes," I said. "She lives with her boyfriend now."

"I imagine the apartment is safe then?"

"As safe as it can be," I assured her. "Don't worry, you'll be fine."

"I'm not worried about me," she said. "You've made two deals in a day and you're going to end up getting fucked by both of them."

The door to the room closed a second later and I brewed myself a cup of coffee and drank it in my Chesterfield, staring at the brick wall. When I was done, feeling completely refreshed (I reminded myself to recommend Nikita's all-night blend) I dressed in my Italian suit, slipped into my best shoes and texted for a taxi.

This may come as a surprise to some, but not to others, that the more *unique* a brothel's services the less they advertise. Brothels are of course illegal in the UK but nevertheless a business must have advertising to attract new clients. This does not apply when what you offer is in demand of the select few who are likely to put the time in to find you.

I doubted myself when the address brought me to a dilapidated house on the outskirts of the city on Ipswich Road. The tall gate was rusted and chained with double loops, the big links and the even bigger padlock practically welded shut with rust. Beyond the gates the house looked forlorn and unvisited, the windows were boarded up on the outside which usually meant listed windows behind them. The driveway was covered in several layers of leaves and the garden had grown to the size of a reasonable swamp.

I looked up and down the street, spying for the tell-tale signs of the folds. Norwich is folded. On the map the city isn't that impressive, fitted as it does neatly in the bulge of Britain's island. But in reality the landmass of the city is astonishing. The reality of it all just crumpled and folded into a smaller space. You could spot them sometimes, when the mind wasn't distracted with the so-called real world.

Have you ever been standing somewhere and thought you'd heard something wrong? Ever smelt something that shouldn't have been there? It's because you know that the other world exists. So does everyone else, even more so now. You know those compilation videos on YouTube of those creepy, unexplained phenomena? You would be amazed at how many of those are real and yet dismissed as fakes by the majority of people simply because they have an already established idea of what the world holds.

I finally spotted what I was looking for, a folded gap near the side of the gate that looked like a hole. A deep, black hole that was big and small at the same time.

"Invitation please," a voice said from inside the gloom.

I peered in closer. "Is that you Billy?"

There was a moment's pause from the hole and then a panicked, "Oh no."

I put my hands on my hips. "Holy cow, it's been ages!" I said. "Aren't you working for Madam Thankeron anymore?"

"No!" the bogeyman grumbled morosely. "What good is a bogeyman who gets hauled up to the house by someone without an invite?"

"Yeah," I sighed. "Good times. Good memories. So you're working here now?"

"Eh, no!" the bogeyman said quickly, his voice bouncing off the inside of his hole. "I, er, I just live here."

"You asked for my invitation," I pointed out.

"Force of habit," he said quickly. "You don't need an invitation to go he– damnit!"

I felt really sorry for the monster. "It's okay Billy,"

"Please don't tell them I told you that!" he pleaded as great gnarled knuckles came out of the hole and clasped together. "I don't want to get fired again and I'm no good at under the beds!"

"Why not?"

"Because futons are so fucking popular at the moment," he snarled angrily. "And these built in wardrobes are cramped and besides the *things* children do when they discover you're afraid of stuffed anim–ah *shit!*"

I bit my tongue to stop myself from laughing. I had to look away though. "I promise I won't tell anyone anything Billy," I assured the monster. "But I do need to get inside."

"But I can't let you," the bogeyman said, with a whiny quality. I noticed the hands had withdrawn back into the gloom of the hole. "I'm supposed to be security here."

"Don't centaurs come here?"

"Oh loads of halfies come here," the bogeyman said offhand. "They get here what they don't get anywhere else."

"Oh do they?"

There was a sullen silence from the hole. I put my hands on my knees and peered in. "You weren't supposed to tell me that either were you?"

"*Plleeeaaase,*" the bogeyman wailed.

"Look I promise I'll keep quiet, this time," I said. "If you get me inside."

"Hop the fence," Billy grunted.

"With Wraith Security?" I said. "I thought you liked me more than that Billy..."

It took the bogeyman a moment or two to decide what he wanted to do. Finally he said, "Okay. I can show you a back way in but you *have* to be quiet and you can't be seen."

"I'm good at that."

"Promise you won't draw any attention to yourself?" he asked.

"Scout's honour," I said, saluting.

"Fine," he said, stepping out of the hole, revealing all ten feet of himself. I looked up at the vast hairy, bejointed monster that leered over me, and he pointed at the hole he had climbed out of. "This way."

I shrugged and ducked into the hole which was now big enough to walk in with space to spare, although Billy had to slouch. Whereas beforehand I could have sworn the hole had been dug through the ground, and that I had seen fine roots growing through the sides, the burrow was now a corridor of brick and mortar. It would have been large enough to permit Billy and a centaur; the recent presence of the latter was confirmed by lumps of centaur droppings that had been deposited in the middle of the walkway. I stepped around them but Billy didn't even notice.

"Billy," I said, "I didn't want to say anything but is that a ribbon in your hair?"

He mumbled a response, "It's black silk, like a gentleman's."

"A very old fashioned gentleman," I pointed out.

"I look regal," he informed me.

I nodded. "And am I mistaken, or have you actually bathed?"

"Only once!" he cried, his knuckles bouncing off the floor. "I've never worked in an establishment with such pretty ladies. At Thankeron's I just stayed at the door, but here I actually escort people to the party. I'm important."

"You bring them this way?" I asked.

"Yes," he said. "But you're not going in the front door like the guests."

Further down the corridor, which wasn't quite halfway judging by how it continued onwards to a very distant point, we came to a green painted door on the left with a crinkle glass window that read STAFF ENTRANCE. Billy opened it for me.

"You follow this corridor down, it'll take you to the servants' quarters and the kitchens. Now just be sure you're not spotted – seriously, I don't want to get into trouble."

I held up my hand. "I'll be discreet."

I stepped into the dark corridor and he closed the door behind me and I heard him muttering unhappily to himself as he walked back to the gate. When he trod in the centaur shit he moaned louder.

10.

Very uneventfully, I walked away from the door deeper into the gloom. It was as black as the inside of an inkwell but Nikita's special blend of coffee had given me a positively chipper feeling. Not to mention it made me feel good that Billy had come so far in life. Last time I saw him he was fleeing from me into the darkened woods that acted as Madam Thankeron's garden, flipping cars and knocking down trees along his way.

I reminded myself that I had to check in on the old girl, see how she was doing. I wondered if she was still angry about me not calling her back. Again.

A short distance away in the dark I heard the clunking of a heavy door being opened and shuffling of footsteps, muffled by either a thin wall or another door, and instinctively I slowed my pace and lowered my stance, preparing for action. Moments later a cord was yanked and a rectangle of light punctured the darkness. A figure passed in front of the glass portion of the door on the other side mumbling some kind of indistinct tune.

I made it to the door before the light cord was yanked again and the room plunged back into darkness. I laid my hand on the door handle, turning it just at the same time the heavier door thunked.

I slipped through into a white corridor with a matted floor. There was the smell of heady meaty stock being brewed and the unmistakable clinking-clonking sound of a busy kitchen, punctuated by pot lids being rattled and people shouting to each other.

Following my nose I sought out the kitchen with the intention of sneaking past it but as I approached a woman in a hairnet and a bloodied apron stepped out and almost bumped into me. I stepped out of the way and allowed her to gain her composure. She looked up at me and frowned. "Sorry..." she began, in the Norfolk manner of preceding any direct question with an apology.

"Can I help you?" I asked, irritably.

"Erm, no," she said. "I'm sorry, I was just going to get some flour."

"Flour?" I asked. "For what?"

"The cake," she said, pointing behind her (I noticed her forearms were covered with sleeves of white and the blood on her apron looked suspiciously like cramapple). "I'm making the cake for dessert."

Now she didn't say cake. She used a very fancy word that sounded more sugary than the dessert itself. I nodded, my frown deepening on my forehead and when she didn't immediately say something else I stepped aside. "Well go on then, don't keep people waiting."

The woman scurried on past and I stalked past the kitchen. Walking past the kitchen was never a problem, you could be a gun toting crazy person but as long as you didn't walk into the kitchen during a busy time of night you wouldn't end up dying as one.

Through a set of double doors at the end of the corridor I found myself on a balcony overlooking a vast chamber. The balcony swept around the entire circumference of the hall and was wide enough for a couple of tables and comfortable looking chairs on which sat the patrons.

"Rakes," I whispered. Hundreds of them, seated at tables in their nappies and gowns, emaciated skeletons in tightly bound skin, as if their skeletons had been vacuum packed into their flesh. Every one of them held onto their IV drip stands like wizards with their magical staffs. Each stand fed their liquid nourishment into their bodies through their arms and all of them were grimly focussed on the events happening below.

It was the destination of whatever the kitchen was busy putting together. Beneath a thin dome of glimmer that probably resembled a ceiling from the other side, dozens of halfies were preoccupied with the act of coupling with human females.

It was deplorable to see. Human waitresses brought in the finest meals to be laid on the long table in the centre of the floor while around the edges women and (I noticed this part with particular biased horror) men were tied over wooden pommels and barrels while centaurs, pans, dracons and minotaurs took them roughly.

The glimmer of the ceiling prevented any sounds from reaching us but the rakes were furnished with ear phones and some of them had the volume up so loudly that I could hear the shrill little screams.

I looked at the rakes sitting around the balcony in their little groups, all withered with their drawn lips pulling their mouths into perpetual toothy grins. I couldn't touch them, the disease that turns people into these emaciated husks also binds them telepathically into a hive and is communicable via touch.

So as they had not noticed me I backed away into the corridor, turned and met an approaching, high speed fist.

11.

A sack was pulled over my head and my wrists were bound with duct tape behind me. I was led like this through the corridors, until a door was opened and I was told to go inside. I shambled forward until the door was slammed shut behind me and I was able to get a rough inkling of the size of the room by the reverberation. I guessed I was in a closet.

I turned immediately to my left and found the wall and started skirting my way across, using the side of my shoe to search out for any obstacles on the ground while my shoulder pressed against the wall, which felt rough and scraped at my jacket sleeve. Rough brickwork and cold.

Like this I went on until I reached the corner and continued on for several feet before I stopped and considered something.

"Hello?" I asked into the dark.

"I was wondering when you were going to realise you weren't alone," Miss Wandilyn said hotly.

"What the hell are you doing here?" I demanded.

"I was following a lead," she explained.

"That is my job," I said.

"I was getting impatient," she said.

"Why are you in here?"

"They caught me and put me in here," she explained. "Then forgot about me. Can you come find me please? I'm tied to this chair."

"Okay hang on," I said. "Did you see the room when you came in? Are there any obstacles?"

"No," she said. "Clear floor space all around,"

In the darkness she would have heard a thunk and a groan.

"Oh, except that anvil."

"*Coorrrr,* that was my shin. Who the hell keeps an anvil nowadays?" I asked, kneeling down so I could manoeuvre my bound hands under my ass, then slipping each of my legs through so that I could pull the sack off my head. The darkness in the room was broken by the vague light coming through the door and it took me a second to orientate myself.

"Can you untie me now?" she asked.

"Can you see in the dark?" I enquired.

"Yeah," she said. "Pretty well. What are you doing?"

I had my hands out in front of me, and had bent my knees and braced myself. For a moment I look like a rugby player planning to take a conversion kick. The duct tape was fastened tightly around my wrists but by angling my elbows out I was able to strain the tape against my wrists which were strengthened by me balling my fists.

I brought my arms back hard, the insides of my elbows hitting my hips with as much force as I could muster. It only took a couple of tries before the duct tape was sufficiently broken for me to wriggle my arms out.

"That was actually quite impressive," Miss Wandilyn acknowledged. "I was sure you were going to break your wrists."

"I saw it on YouTube," I explained, finding her in the dark with my hands. "Oh, my... sorry," I said quickly, withdrawing my hands.

Moments later she was untied and stretching out her legs. I took the chair and tested its weight as a weapon.

"They'll be sending someone in to check on me," I said. "They're probably trying to figure out the best way to get rid of us. It was a Doorman who hit me."

"I thought you would have known all the Doormen in this city," she said snarkily.

"I do," I said glumly, positioning myself near the rectangle of light. "Did you see what they were doing in that hall?"

"No," she said, "I got here earlier today."

"How did you know to come here?"

"My father's wallet. If he had anything he didn't want me to see he kept it in his wallet. He had an old receipt for this place... fairly ratty but still legible. I just walked in easily enough... the bogeyman didn't even see me."

"How did they see you?" I asked.

"I might have walked into their kitchen," she admitted. "The chef saw me and raised the alarm."

Ah, of course, I thought, chefs would even spot Old Forgetfuls if they trespassed into their kitchens.

"It's horrific what is happening here," I said, not wanting to go into details. "And there is something else going on..."

While speaking I was also listening out for approaching footsteps. When I heard them I could tell they were coming our way and whispered, "Get as far back into here as you can."

"There's not much space," she said.

"Then if you feel the need to duck do so," I said. "Just don't hit that anvil."

The door handle rattled and was pulled open by the Doorman who had punched me. I got the advantage on him because at the same time as the door was opening I was swinging the chair. If it had been opened by someone wanting to rescue us I would have been unable to stop the swing, which had been very powerful.

The chair shattered across the Doorman's chin, leaving me with a chair leg in each hand.

The juggernaut swayed back on his heels and blinked. "Ow," he said in a low voice and reached out to grab me.

With a quick movement I slapped the top of his wrist right on the bony joint with one of the chair legs which made him recoil with surprise. I took advantage of the situation and attacked him with as many appropriate *kali* and *escrima* attacks that I could manage until my chair legs were splinters and the Doorman seemed more irritated than actually hurt.

So I kicked him as hard in the fork as I was able.

His face creased and his eyes rolled to the ceiling but he didn't go down. His hands went down to cradle himself and Miss Wandilyn shoved past me, grabbing my wrist and dragging me along.

"Why are you limping?" she asked as we went down the corridor.

"That *hurt* more than the anvil," I complained. Behind us there was finally a thud as the Doorman fell over.

I noticed something in the corridor then. In the corner near the ceiling, it caused me to stop for a second and think of something. "Did you and your father have cameras in your house?"

This in turn stopped her in her tracks and she looked queer for a moment. "No, why?"

"We'll talk about it later."

"How are we going to get out of here?" she asked.

We were in a section of the house shaped like a big square, four identical passageways decorated with Persian carpeting and those random tables with flowers and visitor books. A central courtyard protected beneath a glass ceiling was the central feature. Green palm leaves pressed up against the glass. As we moved down one corridor more Doormen than I would be able to cope with piled into the corridor on the opposite side. Their thunderous steps rattled the floor beneath our feet.

I ushered Miss Wandilyn behind me against the wall and took a position to guard her as best I could, my arms extended to each side as the Doormen rounded the edges. I spotted the angry face of the Doorman I had floored moments earlier who was up on his feet, pitiful bruising marking his bald head.

I felt like a tortoise in a ravine with walls of wildebeest approaching on all sides, yet I didn't have a shell to crawl back into.

I targeted the first of the Doormen as they approached; a calm, machine part of my brain marking targets and potential weak spots. I was certain I would be able to take out at least a couple of them before they splattered me to the wall like a mosquito. Hurt them at least.

Miss Wandilyn wrapped her arms around me from behind and I struggled, thinking that in her final moments of panic the woman had lost control of her disdain for me and had latched onto the most secure object she could reach.

Her hands latched together in front of my chest and the most peculiar thing happened.

The Doormen slowed their approach, bewildered expressions contorting their faces. Not the expressions of men who have seen something disappear because this was not surprise – rather the frustrated expressions of people who have run into a room only to forget what they were here for.

The nearest Doorman was so close I could smell the fabric of his black suit and see the pores in his shaven scalp. On either side of him were similarly dressed and shaped behemoths, blocking both sides in a wall of black. I felt like I was caught in some strange Moses and the Red Sea scenario.

After waiting for their clunky brains to work out why they had been running, they began to disperse, walking away in twos or threes to go do whatever it was that they did when they weren't guarding doors. When I saw the backs of the last of them I gasped and sagged into Miss Wandilyn's arms.

"I thought I'd help you before you got yourself killed," Miss Wandilyn said behind me.

"Of course," I said aloud. "You're an Old Man Forgetful, well an Old Woman Forgetful – a Young Woman Forgetful. They had simply forgotten we were here!"

"Yes."

"That could be very useful," I said, watching the last of the Doormen turn down into staircases before heading to one of the staircases in search of a door to the outside.

"It isn't everything it's cracked up to be," she said in my ear. "Nobody remembers you. You're having a conversation with someone and then they look away and when they look back they don't even know who you are, literally forgetting that you were there at all."

"Sounds lonely," I said, pushing open a staircase door with my foot and peering in. We started down.

"It is," she agreed.

"How many Forgetfuls are there in the world?" I wondered aloud.

"Too many to count," she said. "If you could find them at all... no matter what we accomplish in life, we have no history about us, no stories, no representation. For thousands of years nobody has even known we existed."

I noticed there were more cameras in the staircases. One for every corner. I'd counted three dozen already, growing out of the corners of the building like bushels of bulbs.

We reached the end of the staircase and exited into another corridor where several groups of Doormen stood in small clusters talking to each other in low, gruff voices. We walked right past them and I recognised the doors that led to that hallway; pulling Miss Wandilyn with me I stepped through them and saw that the show was continuing unabated.

"Oh my," Miss Wandilyn said, bringing her hand to her mouth as she saw the gathered rakes, then she witnessed the scene that they were all watching and whispered in a far more different tone. "*God.*"

Things had progressed. New humans had been brought in while the used, spent ones lay around the edges. The fact that these poor people were alive was proof that a body will struggle to survive as long as it can. It made me feel physically sick.

"Disgusting halfies," Miss Wandilyn muttered.

I pointed to the rakes. "It's their fault," I said. "They're the ones who set this up."

"Doesn't mean that they are innocent!" Miss Wandilyn shouted, made brave by her cloak of anonymity. "Look at what they are doing!"

I wasn't listening. I was looking for something. But she carried on with her tirade, "What kind of monster would rape a human girl half to death then leave her on the side lines to bleed and try to push herself back in? What kind of disgusting beast could have the stomach to be so violent?"

I found what I was looking for and, letting go of Miss Wandilyn's hand, I swept across the platform at a rake a little further down that had risen from its table to adjust the sachets of fluid hanging on its IV drip. Hunched over its medication it didn't notice my approach until it was too late and when it did its eyes blossomed and its toothy mouth dropped in a surprised gasp just as the heel of my shoe collided with his chin.

The spinning reverse heel kick had managed to snap the creature's head back and throw its balance onto its heels so that when, continuing my spiralling momentum, I kicked him with a donkey heel kick to the chest, he toppled over the banister. The tubes connecting it to its IV pulled taut and the IV stand yanked across the platform, hit the side and vaulted majestically over the banister.

The rake and his stand and a rain of chemicals hit the glimmer dome and crashed through it to collide with the central table that was bedecked with food.

The halfies downstairs, all of them bred for war, acted like any athletic, powerful warriors would act when a diseased monster crashes through an imaginary ceiling.

They stampeded the hell out of there.

Rakes, having witnessed what I had done, acted. They reared up, possessed by a sudden, starving energy that gave them each the strength of ten men. They snarled and tore their IV drips out of their arms and leapt upon their tables.

Miss Wandilyn appeared at my side and took my hand and as expected the rakes forgot us, while below the halfies were running. There were screams of surprise and roars of anger, as these beasts discovered that their route out was not as easy as their route in.

We left the platform, carefully avoiding the snarling rakes and ran through the kitchen. The chef, who was possessed of eight arms like an octopus, went mental and threw cleavers at us as we ran between his stoves. One of the cleavers hit one of the cooks clean in the face and chopped half his head off, but we were out of the room before the blood had even hit the floor.

The door on the other side led us down another flight of stairs to the arena, where the body of the fallen rake was starting to shiver as it attempted to repair itself. But without its IV drips the creature inside of it was coming out.

This had been what those warrior halfies had been running from. Every Late and Otherwise knew what was inside the rakes.

Meanwhile, I noticed that there were cameras set at intervals around the entire room, just below the glimmered ceiling that now had a massive ethereal hole in the top.

"We have to go now!" Miss Wandilyn cried, tugging on my arm.

The rake's body was now convulsing and its stomach began to distort as something inside coiled and moved. At the same time its body shrank further against its skeleton, sucking itself dry as whatever was inside the belly was growing, bulging upwards like a malignant fast growing pregnancy turning the thing into a particularly unpleasant spider shape.

I backed up, letting the doors swing shut just as the rake's guts exploded.

What came out of the rake is difficult to explain... but it was very much worth running away from.

The stampede of halfies, which included many large creatures with very big hooves, had left a trail of trampled human servants as easy to follow as breadcrumbs. Behind us there was the sound of a million spiders running across the floor while ahead of us was an almighty crash.

We found the biggest hole in the wall where the front door had once existed and exited out into the cool Norwich air and didn't stop running until we had both leapt over the gate.

I landed roughly and only just managed to avoid Billy's massive hand as he tried to slap my head. The bogeyman roared, "I said don't be seen you utter wanker! I'm going to rip your bloody head off you sonofa... oh... um... oh dear, what was I doing?"

12.

The pale light of morning was just nudging the shadows of night out of the city when the taxi stopped outside Miss Wandilyn's apartment in Browser Edge. I saw her off and then caught the same cab back to mine, but the driver forgot that we had made an additional stop immediately and declared that the meter was faulty and asked that I pay only half the fare.

Danielle was curled up on my sofa under a duvet, so small that I wouldn't have seen her if not for the television being on, running through an early morning infomercial about fitness products. I drew the duvet up over her shoulder and went to my room where I fell fully clothed onto my bed. Sleep had me before I had even face planted the pillow.

When I woke, with sunshine coming through the blinds like slices of cheese, the first thing I did was send a text to Danielle. She replied a moment later, *YOU'RE LATE AGAIN.*

I showered, dressed and headed out.

On the way to the office I stopped at Aroma on Upper King Street and found Nikita in her usual merry mood.

"Reginald mentioned you last night," she said conversationally as she made my morning latte. I was leaning on the window counter watching the traffic.

"Oh?" I asked.

"Said something about your past coming to haunt you," she said, posing the obvious question as a statement.

Nikita was a great many things to a great many people. Her modesty kept the truth of her nature from even herself, but there was a reason that she was unable to see the city for what it truly was. Simply because she had nothing to fear from human, Late or Otherwise, locked within her was a power that was untapped and completely unexplored but felt by every creature that came into her presence. It was such that Aroma had become an unofficial sanctuary for all manner of creatures who found solace in the fear that her ignorance created. Everyone wanted to be friends with Nikita, everyone wanted her to be happy. Everyone was terrified of her or her brothers discovering the truth about their abilities. Hell, for some people, her boyfriend included, it was believed that my entry into this world had come about purely so I could be a distraction to her... misleading her from discovering what she was and accidentally turning the city into a crater. I wanted to satisfy her curiosity (which is fortunately not the same as answering a question) but I was afraid I didn't quite understand what she or Reginald meant.

"We all have a great number of things from our past that could haunt us," I said to her. "Any chance he was slightly more specific?"

"Afraid not," she said. "He didn't seem too happy about getting into details about it, as he said it in passing."

Hitting me like a bucket of ice cold water in the morning, an epiphany hit me solidly in the brainpan. I wheeled on Nikita wanting to share it with someone, but out of everyone I knew Nikita was probably the worst person to share it with. She was dating an ogre, an ogre who she believed to be a wealthy businessman and an ogre who shared with me only one other experience which would be enough to haunt me... and him.

"I can't tell you!" I squealed before fleeing the coffee shop and running down the street to my office.

"It's a shirime demon!" I panted, slamming both hands flat onto Danielle's desk.

"Are you sure?"

I counted off points on my fingers. "They look human, they're hardy bastards and they kill with their lady parts."

Danielle frowned. "Don't they have an eyeball in their backsides?"

"Yes, and teeth in their vaginas," I said, counting down another finger. "I got very close to one last year when it tried to kill me."

"I am aware of the story," she said. "Do you think it is the same one?"

"No," I said, too quickly. "She was killed."

"By you?" Danielle asked, with a raised eyebrow.

I shook my head.

She let it drop quicker than I expected and went to her iPad. "Okay, so it may be another shirime demon... what now Mister Detective?"

I played with my tie knot nervously. "I don't know," I admitted. "But it might have something to do with rakes."

Her eyebrows went up. "We have rakes in Norwich?"

"Hundreds of them," I said.

"And you know this how?"

"I, erm, went to that brothel that Mary told us about last night, while you were asleep, and I saw them all watching some kind of show."

"A show?"

"A spectacle more like," I said. "It was horrible."

I described what I had seen and Danielle's face turned grey. I said to her, "Could it be possible that the shirime demon is being paid by the rakes to kill these people?"

"People?" Danielle asked.

"Come on!" I scolded. "They are clients Danielle, you can't let your personal prejudices get in the way of our work."

She blinked and said levelly, "People as in more than one person?"

I smacked my forehead. "We have another client, Miss Wandilyn. She is the daughter of Jason Macadias."

"The Old Man Forgetful?" she asked. "I've read about him."

"You met his daughter yesterday."

"No I didn't... did I really?"

"Yes, her father was killed in the same way as Aggregosh. She found him in the bedroom..."

"What is it?"

"It's an idea," I said. "But I'm probably going to get slapped for it."

The slap that I did receive was a spectacular one. Memorable in fact. It left a blazing handprint, complete with four perfect welts across my cheeks and left my ears ringing.

"Is that a yes or a no?" I asked afterwards, my eyes streaming.

"You are such a pig!" Miss Wandilyn snarled, stalking up and down her living room. "How dare you ask me such a question? Who the hell do you think you are? Bastard!"

"Look," I said, stepping up to her and taking her arms in my hands; I held her for a moment and looked into her eyes (I think they were brown, or maybe green), and said in a soothing tone, "All I asked was if you were fornicating with your father."

When she tried to kick me in the crotch I shook her. "Wandilyn – you paid me to find your father's killer and frankly I have a lot riding on this at the moment so I would like to get this solved pronto. Answer my question... did you and your Daddy do the dirty?"

I sat her down on her sofa and stepped away from her. I didn't feel at all proud about the situation. The woman was still dressed in her nightgown, her hair wet from her morning shower. I stood, silent as a statue, waiting for her to answer. Finally she broke down in tears and admitted it.

"Wow that's gross," I exclaimed before I could stop myself.

"Thank you for your professionalism," she grunted.

"Why?" I asked, wanting very much to wash my hands. "Jason seemed to be so straight-lined?"

"We were the only ones who could remember each other," she explained, in a tone that was so sincere and soft that I had to sit down to listen as she continued. "It happened gradually and we just wanted to be loved. It didn't feel wrong... it felt pretty good actually. He was an incredible lover and willing to do everything."

I went to the bathroom and washed my hands. After, I found her in the kitchen pouring a morning drink.

"How did you know?" she asked.

"When you told me how you discovered your father's body you said 'the' bedroom instead of 'his' bedroom. It didn't sit with me right from the start but I was too slow to pick it up at first."

She necked the alcohol in her glass and slammed it down onto the kitchen counter. "Okay, so you got me. I'm an incestuous whore. Do you still want me as a client?"

"You've already paid," I said. "And I may have already ordered some rather expensive stuff online so it's too late to back out now. I have one other question though. Last night at the brothel I mentioned the cameras and you acted very weird about it."

She shrugged. "Father and I liked to make tapes."

"Oh."

"Nothing hardcore," she defended. "Well, they were, but they were home movies. Don't look at me like that mister, when we're recorded there is proof of our existence. We are real then to the whole world like at no other time."

I frowned, "These tapes of you and your father, were they stolen?"

"No. They are safe. Do you want to see them?"

"No!" I blurted out, stepping away, wiping my hands on my trousers. "Okay I have to go now. I'll be in touch."

"Are you sure you don't want to stay?" she asked, in a tone I was not expecting. "You know that I am a pervert, why not take advantage of it?"

Blind flies could have wandered into my mouth.

"I don't think that would be professional," I mumbled.

"Who is going to remember?"

"Me," I answered.

She smiled. "Good."

I took her on the couch. I mean we had sex but there wasn't much 'taking' to be had. If this book is ever made into a movie, hopefully I'll be depicted as being the man who did the 'taking', who royally fucked Miss Wandilyn, but in truth from the moment she threw me on the couch I didn't have any control of the situation. She took off my clothes with a kind of mania and quickly had me in her mouth.

Fellatio is something that has to be practised and although I didn't want to think about where she had learnt her skills I could not argue against her prowess. She used a lot of spit, slickening up my shaft and using it to massage my head so that my hips bucked in ecstasy. She rolled my testicles in her hands while licking me from my root to the tip. I put my hands behind my head and closed my eyes, enjoying the moment with a zen-like appreciation.

I heard the distinctive sound of a condom wrapper being broken open and when it was not pulled over my cockhead I started to wonder where it had disappeared to – simultaneously I noticed that she was no longer using her hands.

At first I assumed it was an adventurous, cheeky finger pressing against my anus and while I thought it was a little early in the proceedings for that I allowed it for the sake of the 'moment'. But the finger soon became thicker and in my mind's eye, the dark sanctum of my bum region was penetrated by something hard and plastic with extra stimulating nodes pressing against my perineum.

Gods, I thought, *I hope he keeps this out of the book.*

She resumed using her mouth with new vigour and I assumed that while she was great at giving head she was misinformed about what's to be done with a guy's bottom and that some of us don't enjoy the distended fullness that our female counterparts might en–

Then she turned the fucking thing on.

A buzzing like something felt on industrial scale washing machines vibrated inside me and set my bones rattling. It made me cross-eyed and enter a full body stiffness as my mind stopped all processes to focus on this one event. Meanwhile she continued on my shaft – an act that was timed with every downward stroke with the pulsating beat of the prostate massager that was having a temper tantrum inside me.

Twenty-twenty hindsight does beg why I didn't think this was all moving a bit fast but it takes a better man than me to stop a really good blowjob, even if I sounded like a maraca.

The buzzing inside me made me aware of an entire area of my body I was, until now, fairly ignorant of. There was something inside me that I was not acquainted with and was astonished that I had missed it for all these years; an entire section of the orchestra of pleasure that had been, as of yet, ungoverned and unexplored. My scope of music would be forever altered.

With a pop Miss Wandilyn took me out of her mouth and buried her snout into my scrotum, swirling her tongue around that sensitive jewel purse. "How's that?" she muffled.

I groaned in response, letting my body relax into the pulsating buzz from the vibrating toy while her administrations continued with my shaft and jewels. It was a pleasure that I had not experienced yet, not as sudden and peaking as the usual orgasm but longer, building up slower and when she changed the settings and the middle sections of the toy began moving against my innards I stared blindly at the ceiling, more aware of my body than ever before.

"You like that don't you?" she asked huskily, changing her position and climbing on top of me.

With my eyes closed I was able to picture her appearance better than with my eyes open. I sensed smooth, hot thighs against my hips, and a steaming hot oily wetness.

My hands found their way to her legs and stroked up the flesh beneath her robe. The flesh was youthful and hot, like warm silk.

There was a moment of hesitation as the very tip of my shaft pressed against her entrance and then with a gasp she lowered herself onto me and

I slid deep inside her. The sensation brought about an additional tightness to the buzzing device up my ass and it meant that none of the vibrations were able to escape into the air. The effect was to increase the sensations that now I could feel in my skull.

"I can feel you buzzing inside me," she whispered. "It's so fantastic. It's unbelievable. Who would have thought you could be *so* big? Oh my God, oh my God, Donnie, you're the *best* lover I've ever had... I've wanted you to be inside me for so long, ever since we first met, you're my king, you're my lover!"

"Shut up," I said.

"Why?" she asked, still riding me. "You don't like it when I talk dirty to you baby? Are you not a fan of that?"

(FYI: I'm not really, I like the occasional filth but in short spurts, otherwise I like anyone I'm sleeping with to communicate to me in the universal language of good sex, which comprises mostly of vowels, swearwords, exclamation marks and fingernail marks).

I jerked my hips skywards on her downward stride and hit the rounded end of her vagina – she yelped in mid-sentence and was quiet for a moment.

I noticed that she wasn't looking at me either but staring at a point somewhere behind me against the wall.

A part of my mind, the part that was mostly affected by the ninja assassin training I received when I was a child (and the part of my mind that is usually most embarrassed by the other parts) quickly backtracked through my visual memory, scanning every detail of the house that I had noticed as I walked in. The training I had received as a child had affected my brain at the stages of development to give me almost photographic recall of images. Usually I use this to establish the best routes of escape from the houses of important people whose wives I'm banging. But it was useful for moments like this. The interior of the house was modern. Darker shades of paint on the walls to make a warmer feeling to the cold Norwich winters, lots of paintings and photographs on the walls; landscapes, cityscapes and the air freshener.

I turned my head up and peered over the arm of the couch, a movement that caused my hips to rise higher into her. She swore loudly at the ceiling and didn't spot me spying on the air freshener that was positioned on the side table next to a vase of flowers.

Lots of people hide air fresheners next to flowers, but this wasn't an air-freshener. I could see the little black lens of a camera.

"Fuck me!" she shrieked loudly. "Fuck me like the whore I am Daddy!"

It was that, more than being filmed, that ended it for me. I swept her aside onto the couch and disengaged myself fast. A string of her lubrication flung off the tip of my member as I backed away, tripping over the central coffee table and staggering uncontrollably away from it to trip over the other couch. It was quite a spectacle that ended with me lying on my back with my legs straight up. I realised I was still wearing my socks. The stimulator-toy popped out and landed on the wooden floor with a thump and went berserk with its freedom, rattling across the floorboards as it made a break for it.

"Holy shit! Are you okay?!" Miss Wandilyn asked, getting up from the couch.

"Yes, yes," I said, searching for my pants. "I'm sorry but this is wrong. I can't be having sex with a client, it's just not professional."

"Don't be stupid," she said.

"I'm serious, now where are my trousers," I looked up. "Ah. Okay then."

I dressed quickly, careful not to look in the direction of the air freshener, although I realised something about her. Wherever she positioned herself she would have been within the line of recording. Her whole house was probably covered in cameras, hidden in everyday objects and recording her every moment, including those with her own father.

The thought doused the heat of my arousal with a cold splash of reality. Cameras. I had seen so many cameras over the last night... there were cameras at the brothel, cameras at Miss Wandilyn's house. Everything came in threes, I had learnt the strange truth of this. Where would the next cameras come from?

Or was the third place...?

Something about Aggregosh's tent, I hadn't seen anything in there that resembled modern technology save for something that had been put in the ground, those three holes in the ground; about the size of what would be left by a camera tripod.

Miss Wandilyn was still talking but I had completely phased out. I tied my tie and fixed my collar and said, "Look Miss Wandilyn, we can't do this out of respect for your father. Also, I have an entire life that I could lose, I have respected colleagues whose reputation could be damaged by this kind of affair. I won't belittle my professional standing."

"What bullshit," she said, closing her robe and sitting down on the couch, crossing her legs and folding her arms sharply across her chest. "You had better leave then."

I was already walking to the door.

13.

From my office I called Nikita's boyfriend Reginald. The ogre's tone was pleasant enough. "What do you want?"

"I need to talk to you about finding shirime demons," I said.

"What makes you think I know anything about them?"

"You once said that ogres were the only thing that shirime demons feared," I reminded him. "If I remember that was just before you took the shirime demon last year and... disposed of her."

"I know as much as you," he said.

"I know nothing about them," I said. "Aside from the eye in the bum thing and the teeth. That's about it. Why did you think it was a shirime demon?"

"Does it not fit?"

"Oh it fits perfectly," I concurred. "But it isn't the only possibility and don't believe for a second that I buy that you just 'let it slip' to Nikita. What's happened?"

"I heard about the centaur leader's demise," he said.

"Of course."

"The centaurs are looking for someone to declare war at and they are getting itchy. When I found out how Aggregosh died I knew that it was a shirime."

"Why though?" I asked.

"Because of something the shirime demon that attacked you said."

"What did she say to you Reginald?" I asked.

"She said that if she was killed her sister would avenge her and destroy me."

"You didn't think of mentioning this?"

"Don't forget I don't actually like you that much Donnie," he said.

"But nothing has happened to you has it?" I pressed.

"No, but that is mostly because you have been very discreet. Unfortunately it would appear that her sister is now coming after you because she believes you are the one who killed her sister."

I closed my eyes and leaned back. "But why go through Aggregosh and Jason?" I asked.

"Jason?"

"Oh forget it," I said. "Why doesn't she come straight for me?"

"Do you have siblings?" the ogre asked.

"Two sisters."

"And if one of them was killed and you believed you knew who the killer was and wanted to destroy them would you be direct?"

I already knew the answer. I had once had to reclaim the honour of my sister after one of her boyfriends broke her heart and 'disgraced' her. I had overheard her telling my father and I did exactly what any other ten year old baby brother would do. I snuck out that night, while my parents were busy fussing over my sister and walked to the boyfriend's house. Nobody was home but this didn't stop me from deactivating the alarm for the house, picking the front door lock and sneaking in. I found his room easily enough, the only one with magazine posters on the wall of race cars and bikini girls and that distinctive smell of a teenager's bedroom. I spent fifteen minutes pouring fibre glass shavings into all of his shirts, his jeans and his socks, another five minutes using a paintbrush to administer a layer of White Oak Vapour Rub to the crotch areas of his under pants. Not quite satisfied with this I then pressed half a dozen of my mother's sewing needles into his pillows.

From there I crept into his parent's room, where I emptied out her jewellery box of her rings and necklaces, and slipped them into the bottom of one of the socks I had spared from being filled with fibre glass. I stuck the sock under his mattress next to the pornographic magazines he hid from his parents. One of the smaller rings with a beautiful butterfly gem on it, I took into the bathroom and, upon searching for a moment in the laundry basket found a pair of his jeans I recognised as being his and slipped the ring into the back pocket.

I then left, returned home, snuck back into the house unnoticed and went to bed proud of my revenge and assured that I was making the best use of the education my parents were paying for.

It was many years later that I realised that my sister had overexaggerated the boy's crime, that when she said 'disgraced' she had been merely utilising an emotive word as sixteen year olds are prone to do. Also, while the burns and rashes he received from the shavings and the White Oak were devastating to a teenager and took many days to recover from, the rift I had created with implicating him into the theft of his mother's jewels coupled with the ruination that a needle to the eyeball can do to your vision was a bit harder to recover from.

"I know what you mean," I said to the ogre, "I can deal with whatever she can throw at me, but do you know any way I can find out what her name was?"

"Couldn't you ask Lilith?"

"Madam Thankeron and I aren't really talking at the moment," I said. "Besides I don't need to reintroduce another character yet. You're big enough for that."

"She didn't tell me her name Donnie," he said. "Sorry."

"You're not that useful after all," I said. "If you don't hunt the shirime then what the hell does?"

"Find a winchikari then," he said.

We both hung up at the same time and I put my elbows on the desk to hold up my throbbing head.

Danielle knocked on the door and opened it within the same motion and said, "Gregore has been in contact with the embassy, he is still waiting for your response," she said. "Any progress?"

"I reckon so," I said, "Could you do me the favour and call the Authorities?"

The Norfolk Constabulary manages the policing of the county's cities, including Norwich. Like the City Council they also have branches involved in the policing of the Late and The Otherwise. Although not official, the Authorities were simply there to provide law and justice when the natural order of things didn't manage it. Ultimately, they were coppers.

The person who arrived at my office appeared human. In most ways at least – average height, if not on the slightly short side, wearing jeans, boots, a blue and black checked lumberjack shirt and a black denim jacket. He showed me his ID with a stylish flourish.

"My name is Inspector David Box," he said. "And what do you want?"

"Good to meet you Inspector," I said standing and shaking his hand. "But I wasn't expecting you to come to the office. I asked my assistant to make an appointment to come visit you."

"I was curious," he said. He had the face of a man who spends a lot of time in the sunshine and his accent was foreign but I couldn't place it. Then again, purgatory is filled with people who have been waiting for a long time to leave. I offered him a chair and he took a seat, continuing, "I have been waiting for an introduction with you since your title was changed."

I blushed. "I didn't realise my position title was taken so seriously?"

"Shall we say that you make an impression in whatever role you sit," he said. "Are you calling yourself a Private Investigator?"

"Possibly," I said. "Or detective, haven't really given it much thought, I've been trying to help."

The inspector spread his hands. "Do you have private clients?"

"One private client," I said. "Aside from the Aggregosh case, which I was asked to be involved with when I was still acting Ambassador."

"Well," he said helpfully. "Private Investigator does make for a better sound. Nevertheless, I wanted to meet you personally and explain that I will be your liaison with the Norfolk Constabulary. To properly bring people to justice you need to have the proper channels to the Authorities so that we can make an arrest and a case. Of course, not all of your clients are going to need the involvement of the law. However in circumstances where they do you'll do well to keep my number."

"Understood."

His eyes looked down at my throat for a second and with such a focus that my hand went up to check that everything was alright there. His gaze met mine again and he asked, "Why did you want to make an appointment with me? Have you made progress?"

"I haven't come to a conclusion yet. Do I need to divulge details to you?"

"Not if you think it's going to damage your big finale," Box said. "I've heard how you like to have a big climax. Were you planning on coming to the yard to tell me that you *hadn't* made progress?"

"No, of course not," I said, "I mostly wanted to meet you and to ask for access to your database."

Box shrugged. "Of course we will give you help where we can," he said. "It is important that we find who Aggregosh's killer is and fast, the centaurs are not famous for their patience."

"Last year a shirime attacked me in my home," I told him. "She was killed but I need to know the name of her sibling. A sister, I believe."

Box took out a notepad from the pocket of his jacket and with a stub of a pencil started scribbling notes. "Shirime are very elusive," he said. "It is why they make such good assassins. Do you have her name?"

"She was trying to kill me," I said. "I didn't have the time to stop and ask."

"Do you have a description?"

I gave it: straight red hair, perfect skin and beautiful eyes. Except for the eyeball she had sticking out of her bum.

His pencil scratched in the notebook. "Did she have any acquaintances?"

"Yes," I said. "A barman who tried to murder Madam Thankeron at her home last year."

"He caused the flooding of her property if I recall," he said – his eyes went from his pad up to mine. "You were involved in that?"

I kept my mouth sealed, not feeling comfortable telling the policeman how many people I had killed in the span of a couple of days. I did add, "The barman said that he knew the shirime demon. I had the impression that he knew her... intimately."

More scratching notes.

"I have read some detective novels," I commented. "The police usually aren't so... accommodating."

"Oh we aren't usually," he said, putting the notepad away. "But you know, you're special and all that."

He said that he would get the information to me as soon as it was available and left the office.

Danielle walked in with a fresh coffee and a plate of sandwiches. "Are you hungry?" she asked.

I wasn't, but she had never made me sandwiches before and it felt rude to decline. She put them on the desk between us and sat down in the seat where Box had just sat. She put her hands in her lap.

"Is everything okay?" I asked.

"I wanted to thank you," she struggled. "For saving my life last night. I haven't been very kind to you and I just wanted to say that I appreciated it."

"You don't have to thank me for saving your life," I said. "Anyone would have done it."

"Yes, but it was you," she said.

I didn't know how to take that, so I bit into one of her sandwiches and chewed it.

She didn't leave and when I was done with the sandwich I said, "What is it Danielle?"

"I feel awkward saying this, but I wanted to know if you fancied going for a drink tonight?"

"A drink."

"Yeah," she said cutely. "I thought we could go out to the new club that's opened up in Tombland? It's got a great view of the cathedral."

"It's a bit sudden," I said. "I thought you didn't like me?"

"You don't know everything about women," she said. "If you like I don't mind paying..."

I held up a hand. "No no, I'll pay, don't be absurd. If I take a girl out I'll definitely pay."

"So you're taking me out tonight?"

"Of course."

"Brilliant, shall we meet there at 8?"

"Absolutely."

Delighted, she left the office and I replayed the entire conversation in my head, trying to work out what had just happened.

14.

When I arrived at the club in Tombland, a corner that was one of the oldest in the city and home to a labyrinth of narrow corridors and alleyways unknown by the common person, I found Danielle at the bar sipping a brightly coloured cocktail. Tight fitting blue jeans, a black lace blouse, a brown leather jacket and cowboy boots made her almost unrecognisable to what I had seen in the office. Her short hair was styled in a hip fashion and she had dark mascara around her eyes which made them shine.

"You're late," she said when I joined her.

"I didn't want to disappoint," I said. "Shall we grab a table?"

We were seated on the second floor in a private nook of the club at a window overlooking the cathedral grounds. The rum was very good and the location very fitting but Danielle was slow on conversing, very awkward and unwilling to start. I decided to take the lead.

"Can I say that you look very nice tonight," I said.

"Thanks," she said with a smile.

"I would say beautiful but I don't want to use that line too soon," I added.

She laughed and asked, "Why not?"

"I'll probably be late again for something and need to be able to have an ace up my sleeve," I explained. "It is strange to see you out of your work clothes."

"This is how I usually dress," she said.

This led into the conversation about our lives outside of the office. It was peculiar that she knew so much of my life and my past. Having been assigned to me she had of course been given my bio, but apparently couldn't reconcile the man on paper to the man she had worked for.

"You are an actual ninja assassin?" she asked.

"I didn't graduate as one," I reminded her.

"You were expelled from the school?"

"They expelled me after I left," I corrected. "They didn't have the chance to physically expel me. I moved to Britain, lived in a few places, had a couple of adventures then I moved to Norwich."

"Is that when you became the Ambassador?"

"I was here for a couple of years before that happened," I said. "I don't know what it says in my paperwork but it was all a bit improvised when I started. I was invited to a number of parties, met some strange people and started getting paid to do it. I made assumptions because it was all very badly managed."

"Hence why I was assigned to you," she said, sipping her cocktail in a self-satisfied kind of way.

"Yeah," I said. "Thinking back it all seems unreal at times."

"Do you like Norwich?"

"It's an adventure," I said. "But it's all a mystery to me. I used to not care that I didn't know what I was doing, all I cared about was that I was getting paid to do whatever I liked. I don't think I was a good Ambassador."

"Good thing you changed then," she said. "I was wrong, Private Investigator does suit you better. It gives you an edge."

I smirked, "Do you like the edge?"

"I won't lie, it is pretty sexy," she acknowledged, then blushing, returned to her drink.

"What brought you to Norwich?" I asked.

"You," she said, "The assignment. I mean I've always lived in the city but not this part of it. I grew up about a hundred miles away in an elf colony."

"That must be nice,"

"Bit boring," she said, "So I was eager to come here. The assignment was an exciting one - you come with a bit of a story."

"I daren't imagine," I said.

"They say that you know what women want,"

"You make it sound like I'm some kind of woman whisperer,"

She laughed, "Well, is it true?"

"I just do whatever I want," I said, "And try to be polite about it."

She let her gaze linger as she sipped her cocktail. We had already been drinking quite a bit, I was on my fourth rum and ginger ale and she had been keeping up with me with her cocktails, which had interesting euphemistic names and strange, luminescent colours.

"Do you know what I want?" she asked.

"I have no idea," I admitted.

"You must have some idea," she pressed, rolling her straw between the pad of her thumb and forefinger.

"Oh I have plenty of ideas," I said, "But I'm not *that* good a detective,"

"Oh you're better than you think," she purred.

"Maybe," I said, "Do you want to get out of here?"

"Yes," she said.

Halfway back to mine Danielle pulled me into a shop's darkened doorway and pulled on my jacket lapels to get me down to kiss her. It was a tender kiss, her lips soft and her tongue pressed tentatively against me, teasing my own out. She was so short though that I had to bend double to kiss her, so I reached down, took her rump in my hands and lifted her up.

Without hesitating she wrapped her arms around my neck and her legs hooked around my waist, her ankles locking in the small of my back. The doorframe of the shop rattled as I pressed her against it and our kiss became very much harder. Her lips crushed against mine and her tongue explored my mouth with an almost predatory eagerness.

Weighing almost nothing I contemplated just carrying her back to mine like this but stopped the kiss abruptly instead.

"What is it?" she asked.

I didn't know. But my hackles were up, that assassin part of my mind had noticed something

144

and was still trying to explain it to other parts of my brain, "We're not alone," I said, putting her down.

I peeked out beyond the doorway, looking up and down the deserted street. The street curved down, in the Norwich fashion, old and new buildings right next to each other, ancient unseen buildings hidden between the gaps, the gigantic remnant of the Norwich wall stretching out directly in front. The pale yellow street lamps cast just enough glow that the heavy shadows seemed to swirl around the edges of light like inky soup.

"What is that smell?"

It reached me a second later, a repugnant stench of decomposition. Greasy yet fuzzy, rotting meat mixed with turgid fruit, it made me wince like a punch to my nostrils.

The smell may have reached Danielle first but the screech was heard by both of us at the same time: The unmistakable moaning wail of the same creature that had tried to catch us outside of the city.

"The winchikari," I said.

Danielle's hand urgently grasped my arm, "It followed us back?"

"Yeah," I said, "Frankly I'm glad."

"What do you mean?"

"It's all getting a little heavy with characters at the moment," I explained, "This was supposed to be an easy read."

"Are you having a stroke?" she asked through her teeth, "You're not making any sense."

I ignored her, put my hands out on the brickwork on either side of the door and did my best to listen.

There was a lot of life in the city, ironic considering Norwich's position as Purgatory, but in whatever its form, Late, Lost or Otherwise it teemed and foamed around the city like bubbles in a freshly run bath. All of it seemed to be currently holding its breath.

The devil had warned me that it would follow me, I hadn't really been paying attention. I've dealt with devils before and usually they are full of empty promises and falsehoods. I thought he had just been playing to the humour.

Danielle kicked my ankle, "What are we going to do?" she asked.

"Well, I'm going to take you back to mine and put your over my knee," I said, rubbing my leg. "But first I'm going to have to get us away from the demon monster that's following us."

She muttered something under her breath.

Mentally I mapped out the quickest route back to mine. We'd be safe there. My apartment had been armoured with more security than any other household in the city, pigeons sometimes spontaneously exploded when they landed on my windowsill. If I could get us there we'd be safe.

There was another shriek, closer now, reverberating down the twisted alleyways as if daring me.

"Danielle, you're an elf right?" I asked, "Can't you do something?"

"Like what?" she asked.

"Magic or something," I said, "You know, spells and sympathetic hocus pocus,"

She kicked me in the ankle again.

The next shriek was closer yet and had me pressing us both back into the doorway. I turned around and clapped a hand over Danielle's mouth to stop her from saying anything and twisting into the doorway corner I held her there just as a shadow passed in front of the nearest street lamp.

The smell was overbearing, the kind of redolent putrescence that you can smell in your eyeballs. The winchakiri passed into view, walking awkwardly across the pavement only three metres in front of the doorway. So close that we could see the wet, rotting flesh that covered its long, suspension crane arms. The body of the driver had fully joined with the demon, the seam of flesh indistinguishable, the body itself was shrivelled with dirty rags hanging off it, flexing on every step like a convulsive hand.

The demon's rotten, broken pumpkin face was searching the road, making a wet, sniffing sound as it tried to smell us.

It came to a complete stop directly in front of the doorway; this action made the wrists that it walked on crack like broken bones grinding against each other. The fingers were long and gnarled, the nails blackened and broken. This was just the start of the broken visage that this monster was, I felt Danielle physically recoil in my arms and I held her fast.

Bells from the cathedrals in Norwich, the two major ones that everyone knew and the dozens of others dotted around the city that were Otherwise started tolling, the deep chimes rumbling across the streets in a tide. The demon flinched as it heard them, recoiling slightly from the sound and hissing into the air.

It turned half circle so that its back was to us and I saw up and down its haphazard spine the remnants of the other creatures it had absorbed. There were shapes in the black and grey flesh, pressed up against its parchment skin, the definite visages of faces.

As the bells continued to toll one of these face shapes opened its eyes, milky white and blind but filled with terror, it looked around desperately. Its mouth opened, a gash upon the blackened skin, strings of flesh connecting what would be its lips in front of black gums and rotted teeth.

"Is someone there?" It whispered into the night, at us. *"Is someone there? I'm alive, I'm alive... please, please help me."*

My God in Heaven, I thought in horror.

The winchakiri made a wet sound and swung its head to the left and the right as the bells continued to toll their late hour.

"Please, help me," the face pleaded, *"I'm alive. My God, I'm alive and I'm aware. I can't move, but I can feel... I can feel everything! You have to help me. Please."*

I recognised the details of the face suddenly and my stomach dropped, it was the driver. The taxi driver, his head too far from his body to be connected but he was alive, what purpose other than creating suffering could this serve?

"I want to see my family!" the blind driver continued to plead, *"I want to see my wife and my girl, they don't know where I am. Where am I? Please. Help me."*

On the last word the winchakiri's right limb shot backwards with astonishing speed. My body acted on reflex and swept sideways, drawing Danielle against me, as its lengthy arm punched a hole clean through the heavy wooden door.

Turning its pumpkin head, it followed the length of its arm and had a moment of confusion as it drew its limb from the doorway; for it had missed the prey it had been certain was there.

Meanwhile, with Danielle in hand we had left the doorway, moving out of its line of sight and fleeing down the adjacent gap that Danielle had found between the two buildings.

I was amazed that she had located it for even I hadn't seen it. It was a narrow, claustrophobic alleyway between two sheer walls of old brick that she could run down, but I had to go down sideways. Seconds after we entered there was a murderous shriek of rage as the winchakiri found our escape route and tried to follow. Too large to get through it, the creature scrabbled at the entrance before pulling away from it and vanishing from view.

The gap was the length of a building but when we came out of it the Norwich Castle, which is the highest point in the city, was directly in front of us and facing the wrong way. Surrounded by dark and foreboding warehouses and sprawling brick factories I realised we had come out at the other end of the city. I turned around and went back to the gap but found that it was only a centimetre thick, a dark line in the brick work that I couldn't even get a finger through.

"No closer to mine," I said, putting a hand upon the brickwork.

"Farther away from that monster though," Danielle pointed out.

"How'd you do that?" I asked.

"Otherwise magic," she said, "You did ask what I could do after all."

I straightened up my jacket, "Shall we get a taxi back to mine then?"

"Yours?" she asked.

"It's safer there," I reminded her, "It's got protection, nothing can get over the threshold unless I invite it in."

"Well, to be honest mine is closer," she said, "It's why I brought us down here."

"You live in Cotton Mill?"

"That's right," she said, "Come on, it's only five minutes from here."

Cotton Mill was a section of the city that had once been devoted to the thriving manufacturing trade of cotton and other textiles. Having fallen on hard times these warehouses were shut down, gutted and converted into some of the fanciest and above all expensive residences available in the city.

As we walked out of the factory area I noticed several pallets of concrete, bricks, piles of cement bags and stacked up steel girders. There were other signs of recent traffic, of people wearing work boots and machinery being used.

"Are these being converted to residences as well?" I enquired.

"Yes, they'll be changed to apartments, mostly two and three bedroomed apartments with balconies onto the river, but there will be one or two large studio apartments too."

By this time her hand had slipped into mine, so tiny that she couldn't fit my fingers fully behind hers, so she just gripped a couple of mine.

"I bow to your prescience," I said.

"What do you mean?" she chuckled.

"You know so much about this city," I said, "That gap, these factories, it's all very impressive."

She laughed, "Haven't you worked it out yet?"

"Worked out what?"

"You really don't know who I am do you?" she asked, as we rounded a corner and joined a main walking promenade of cobble stoned, chain linked fences, firelit lamps and manicured bushes all in front of the glass panelled foyer to CottonEdge Haven.

"Who are you?" I asked, not going another step.

"Come on," she urged, drawing me to the glass doors with a hand.

As we approached the Wraith Security appeared, no more than a swirling in the available shadows, like an indistinct smoke that you could only *just* see lurking in the corner of your eye, they dulled down into the darkness once they recognised who she was.

Behind the front desk stood the night clerk, a very straight-backed man with thin black hair slicked away from his forehead and the most precise moustache I had ever seen. Dressed in a three piece suit he stood behind the counter with such a touch of regality that I felt myself straighten up right away.

"Ah Miss Kincade, good evening to you, how are you?" the man asked in an accented tone as precise as his bowtie.

"I'm very well Oliver," she said, hurrying passed him to the elevators.

"Danielle Kincade," I said once inside the elevators, "You're Danielle Kincade?"

She bit her bottom lip, "I might be,"

I collapsed against the side of the elevator, "Holy shit,"

"Are you okay?"

"Well I've just found out that the person who I ask to get my coffee is the daughter of the wealthiest property developer in the city!"

She shrugged, "I don't let it affect my work ethic," she said.

The elevator reached the top floor and opened up onto a single apartment that stretched across the entire building. While technically a studio apartment it took three concrete pillars to hold up the ceiling and three blazer lights to cast enough illumination onto the balcony at the front. I lingered in the elevator.

"Come on, what's wrong?" she asked.

I timidly stepped out of the elevator and stared around, gobsmacked. The timber floorboards were so thick as to feel like granite. Bare brick walls were adorned with grand landscape paintings of cities and mountains, the furniture included thick leather sofas and beanbags, the kitchen was black granite, lit up with hanging light bulbs. There was the smell of pine in the air. Danielle went to the kitchen and opened up a cupboard filled with bottles of alcohol.

"It's... a big place," I said dumbly.

"Does it really bother you that I live here?"

I didn't want to say yes, because it's unbecoming for a man to reveal he's jealous of where a woman lives. But yes. It bothered me.

"If it helps," she said, pouring some rum into some tumblers, "I don't own this place. It's my father's, he owns the building."

It didn't help much.

"Well, he owns the block," she added, bringing over the drinks.

The Kincade family were notorious for a number of reasons. They were a well-known family name, owning over half of all the properties in the city and catering to providing

155

business, retail and residential premises for human, Late and Otherwise. Like a cloud in the sky they covered borders indiscriminately and like a cloud, were just as unreachable. Nothing was known about the Kincades. They were genuinely untouchable.

"The Kincades are elves?" I asked, looking around for somewhere to sit. I followed Danielle to the sofas and while she curled into the three seater corner, tucking her small feet under her, I sat down into a single seater.

"Yes," she said, "We're elves."

"Um, I'm sorry about the whole saying I was going to put you over my knee thing," I said.

"Oh don't worry," she told me, "I'm still going to let you, but I wanted to do that here rather than at yours."

I sipped the rum. Holy shit, it was good.

15

A silence, more awkward than the silence felt at the Last Supper after Judas kissed Christ's cheek, descended upon us. I was looking around the apartment imagining Danielle rising every morning at the crack of dawn and getting into the office and waiting for me to pull myself in through the door. I felt intensely embarrassed. Her father probably owned the building I lived in!

"This place is very big," I said.

"You should have seen the place my sister had," she said.

There was something in her tone, I reflected on it, "Oh, where is she now?"

"She was Late," she said, "But didn't stay in the city for too long before moving away."

"Do you have any other siblings?"

"No," she said, "Just me and my dad at the moment."

I drank some more of the rum. It tasted really, really good.

Danielle ran her fingers through her hair, "I must look like a mess,"

She didn't. On the contrary she looked unbelievably good. I noticed how despite how small her features were she had a fairly square jaw which highlighted the height of cheekbones and the delectable shape of her mouth. Beneath her slender eyebrows her fiercely blue eyes seemed to shine. She moved her legs out from under her.

She stood up, her eyes not leaving mine and as she approached me a rush of blood left my brain and poured into another head.

"I think I'm ready for my spanking now," she said.

She put a hand on each of my knees and spread them. I was aware that some time had passed that I had not been aware of because now she was undressed, standing in black lace panties and a bra that revealed that while her small, round breasts were secured in the bra, her nipples were hard. Everything about her was screaming sex, every corner of her flesh seemed to beckon to my engorged crotch, even her navel and the small indent above her belly button; was a sexual orifice that demanded attention.

She went to her knees in front of me and said, "Are you going to spank me or shall I take the lead?"

"I don't think this is a good idea," I slurred, "That monster could find us here."

"Relax," she said, "The building is guarded, remember?"

She took my glass away from me and put it onto the table. Another moment of time-lapse occurred because suddenly I was aware of a heat around my member. My pants were around my ankles and I was inside her mouth, her nose pressed hard against my lower abdomen at the root of my penis. Her body gyrated for a second as she choked herself on me then upon the second convulsion she drew back with a gasp.

"Wow," she said, heaving for breath.

I put my head back against the cushion of the sofa and stared up at her ceiling at the light directly above me. The blood that was stiffening my penis had also made it more sensitive than usual and I had to mentally concentrate on not climaxing under her precision and enticing handling. The corners of my vision were blurring with purple haze and my pulse was a bass drum in my ears.

"I've always wanted to do this," she said.

I was grateful that the light above me wasn't on, because its glare would have hurt my eyes.

But it didn't look like a light at all. It was a glass bulb. Like a bubble in the ceiling.

I was drugged.

It came as a distant realisation, like a brief flash of light cast by a lighthouse in the mists. It didn't really strike me but just became an accepted reality by a drugged mind.

She had drugged the rum.

I felt Danielle's hand against my suddenly bared chest as she straddled my lap and her fingers encircled my member and rubbed the hardened bulb of my head against her fleshy folds.

I was hit by a flood of sensory pleasure, the sensation brought me to the very edge of climaxing but did not let me crest that wave. The drug in my system brought me right to the edge of satisfaction, teasing me, tantalising me right at the edge.

But this wasn't right.

Why had Danielle drugged me?

Still staring at that non light on the ceiling Danielle leaned into my neck as if to kiss it, but it felt like her cheek pressed against my throat and in a single sweep she descended upon me.

In a blink everything, the whole cosmos, descended to a single length of eight and three quarter inches (*pfft), in the darkness of eternity it was the singularity of the pre-universe. A hot, wet column of sensory distinction in an otherwise black and empty space.

"That feels good," I whispered.

She didn't respond, just pressed her cheek further into my neck. Nuzzling me in response, both hands running through my hair, her nails raking down my scalp. Slowly she drew her hips up.

The drugs took on a different effect, my body may have felt like a loose tent around an engorged, quivering tent pole but the flesh in my body, the muscles, began tensing, became hot and feverish. My body was responding to the drugs, fighting against the dullness by flooding my system with adrenaline.

She plunged her hips down again, slamming down so hard that I cried out in pleasure but she made no verbal noise. All that I heard from her was a muffled snort through her nostrils that, as out of place as it sounded, was still highly erotic. But anything would have seemed erotic in my current mindset.

A red edged mist descended over my vision and everything became sharp edged, angry. A beast mind inside me uncoiled with joy as it was called by my body to fight against the drugs.

It was the beast inside that made me grab her hips and it was the beast that made me, upon her next upward draw to grab her buttocks and slam her down upon me with such anger that she jerked backwards away from me, turning her face up to the ceiling in what would have been a cry of pleasure/pain- but no sound could come out because she no longer had a mouth.

It was gone. In its place was a white sheet of flesh as smooth as the flesh of her buttocks. There was nothing there, no indentation of teeth or lips, just a blank sheet of flesh leading from her petite nose to her chin. Her eyes were squeezed shut at the surprise of my deep penetration and I believe it was that which saved me.

My hands hit her hips and shoved her away from me with such a force that she flung backwards butt first, her head flying forward and her eyes wide with surprised rage. Instead of a cry of surprise what I heard was the distinct *gink* of teeth coming together hard.

Danielle hit the coffee table hard and for a moment I sat on the couch staring at my penis, which had missed being bitten off by only a split second.

"You're the killer?!" I shouted.

On the hard oak coffee table Danielle, on all fours like an animal, turned around and pushed her rear out towards me. A woman assuming this position is usually my favourite thing in the world but this time from what should have been a petite inward knot of flesh was a bulging red eyeball with a dark pupil, and where the neat packaged flowered lips of her vagina should have been were instead a row of teeth, snarling.

I leapt from the sofa, forgetting that my trousers were around my ankles and hit the floor hard for the second time.

She leapt at me from the coffee table but I drew up my knees, my trousers pulled inside out around my shoes and my heels took her weight for only a second before I pushed away with as much strength as I could manage and she went airborne.

Light like a bag of sugar, Danielle landed somewhere on the other side of the sofa.

I struggled to pull my trousers right and had just pulled them up over my legs when she came around the sofa, running backwards at me, her angry red anus eye glaring at me, her toothed vagina wide and gnashing.

Driven by the fear of imminent castration and the benefit of the sofas being so large I managed to pull my trousers up the rest of the way and scrambled to my feet just as she kicked out her legs, hitting me squarely in the chest.

Staggering upwards I felt the beast inside me shove its way into the driver's seat and I lost control.

Danielle turned around to face me, those beautiful eyes now glaring with anger and with her claws out she leapt at me and met my fist full on in her face. If her teeth had still been where they belonged I would have sent them skipping across the floor boards.

"You almost got me!" the beast said through me, as I adjusted the raging erection in my pants, flattening it to the left. "Is that how you killed Aggregosh? Is this how you killed Jason?"

"Who the fuck is Jason?" she shrieked from between her legs, attacking again.

With the aim of getting me within biting distance she attacked bodily, like an animal, flinging her weight against me and slashing with finger nails and toenails, sharp like talons. That she tried it at all made me certain she hadn't expected the drugs to have the opposite effect on me. The beast kicked out with my leg, catching her as she was just leaving the floor with a powerful snap that didn't push her backwards but rather condensed all the power of my leg into a single spot about six inches between the target. Her arms curled around her body and she dropped to her knees only an inch away from where she had been.

"You were the killer the whole time?" I growled, circling around her, "You played me. You were working with Miss Wandilyn and you're recording this whole thing for her!"

"Who is Wandilyn?" she coughed, groaning. "You utter wanker."

"You can't remember her," I said, but the beast was controlling everything I was saying.

Danielle's rear lifted again, the red eye furious and she ran, crouched, over to the kitchen. I followed her, taking my time. The beast would not be rushed.

A drawer was opened and there was a rattling of cutlery. Danielle leapt onto the kitchen counter, knives in her hands, "You murdered my sister!" she screamed and threw a steak knife at me.

I snatched it out of the air. "Your sister was sent to kill me!"

"You *gave* her to an ogre!"

"Ah, so you know about that?"

She threw the rest of the knives in quick succession. I caught another one and dodged the others. The beast was still in control and every time I dodged one of the blades I advanced closer to the kitchen counter.

I threw both knives at the same time in a double throw, my ambidextrous training combining with the accuracy of the world class assassin I was. The blades hit her in the shoulders and a second later I delivered a round house kick that swept her feet from under her. She dropped onto the kitchen counter with a thud.

"Is that all you got?" the beast asked.

Her knees parted wide and her vaginal mouth opened, the teeth widening in a snarl – in that yawning hole I saw what I thought was a tongue, swirling in the depths but it shot out at me. A long, fleshy tentacle of bright pink with a harpoon like stinger at the very end - it would have ploughed into my chest had I not caught it in mid-air and slowed it down.

Slimy and glistening, it had the consistency of a long sausage, with chords of muscles working through it. Danielle held onto the counter with her hands and her feet, her blue eyes glaring at me from over her jiggling breasts while her hateful red brown eye glared at me from between her spread buttcheeks. She tried to recall the harpoon but my grip was hard. From the dark harpoon, scorpion tail tip there was a squirt of ejaculant that landed splotted on my shirt.

The beast roared with an unquenchable rage that my shirt had been sullied and my fingers curled tighter around the appendage. I pulled with all my strength, threatening to pull this shirime bitch inside out if I had to and when her grip on the kitchen counter's edge failed she smashed her head against the counter top on the way off it.

I hauled her by her harpoon appendage, running backwards to get the momentum and swung her by this internal weapon of hers like a cat by its tail, managing to swing her around in a three hundred and sixty degree angle until she met one of the pillars holding up the ceiling. The column of stone didn't even move, didn't even break, there was just a painful dull thud.

She collapsed onto the ground in a heap of limbs.

The beast wasn't done though. Taking one of the knives that she had thrown at me I pinned the harpoon appendage into the floorboards, an action that brought about a surprised, choking cry of pain from Danielle. She tried to scrabble away from me, her finger nails digging into the floor boards as I pulled her by the appendage towards me.

When she was near I punched her hard, rattling her head and flattening her to the boards. On her front, I put my hand into a handful of her hair and smashed her face against the boards, then with the other hand I unzipped myself. The drug fuelled erection sprang out of the front of my trousers and the red eyeball in her anus blinked wide as I positioned myself for entry.

"Okay, you can stop,"

The woman's voice had been expected. Upon hearing it I let Danielle go and stood, struggling to fit my pulsating erection into my trousers before zipping myself up. I pulled the knife out of the floorboards and the shirime's harpoon appendage withdrew. It was a panicked movement and when it had fully withdrawn the vaginal mouth disappeared from Danielle's crotch and soon her mouth had returned to her face and her red eye had been sucked back inside herself. What remained, a small woman, climbed to her feet, staring at me with bare rage. Keeping the knife in hand I looked over at Miss Wandilyn, who was standing at the kitchen counter with a gun pointing at me.

"I was wondering if you were going to arrive in time," I said, feeling the beast seething inside me, "I was almost going to go too far."

"I think many people would think you already had," the forgettable woman said, "Isn't it customary for the hero to show mercy?"

"She killed Aggregosh," I said, "She killed your father."

"He deserved to die," Wandilyn said.

"Who, Aggregosh or your dad?"

The gun didn't move, but she said, "My dad. You idiot... I didn't trust him and I felt that he might have been unfaithful to me, so I tested him. Got the shirime demon to seduce him and he failed to live up to my expectations."

I recoiled faintly from the manner in which she said all this, "You are totally insane."

"It draws in the audience," she said, nodding to the bubble in the ceiling.

I slapped my forehead when I realised, "Oh of course, it's a camera! So, are the rakes watching this?"

"They are some of my clients," she explained, "We have a very diverse audience Donnie. Millions around the world paying us every month to watch us."

"Is this all for the show?" I asked.

"Like I said," Miss Wandilyn explained, "being on camera makes me real. Nobody remembers me otherwise," she nodded to Danielle beside her.

"That isn't my Danielle is it?" I asked, pointing with the blade at the shirime demon.

"No," Miss Wandilyn revealed, "This is Edna. The sister of the shirime assassin you fed to an ogre last year. Edna took Danielle's place while you and I were at my brothel."

Edna said, "I'm surprised you didn't work that out? Why would Danielle be romantically interested in you?"

"Ouch," I said, "I know that I killed your sister- blah blah- but is Danielle alive?"

Edna's face changed. The bones beneath the skin reformed until she looked like a completely different woman. Even the shape and positioning of her eyes shifted: I was impressed, it was very smoothly done and just another thing about the shirime that I had learnt.

"We would not be stupid enough to kill a member of the Kincade family," Wandilyn said.

I sagged, "Oh for Heaven's sake you mean that Danielle is *actually* a member of the Kincade family?"

The two women exchanged a glance and then Edna asked, "Is that really what you care about?"

"She makes my coffee and arranges my diary," I said, "I feel like an idiot. I was hoping that this was your place."

Wandilyn waved it away, "Back to the point. I was in the middle of explaining everything to you."

"Oh a villain's monologue," I said, "Yeah, that would be handy if you could explain everything to me. So what is this show that I'm starring in?"

"You're not the star," Wandilyn assured me, "You're just a character that interests enough people to guarantee an extended audience. This is all about me you see. I am the star."

"So why did you have Aggregosh killed?" I asked.

Non-descriptively, Wandilyn's expression hardened. It was an expression I recognised instantly as a man, a woman bearing it is usually worth stepping away from and potentially hiding behind the furniture.

"He spurned me," she said.

"I beg your pardon?"

"Three years ago Aggregosh and a gang of his finest ventured into the city and started making a fuss. I saw him and was enthralled. His size, his muscles, his utterly massive hooves... I wanted him."

I made brief eye contact with the shirime demon at Wandilyn's side. The creature gave a little shrug as if to say, *What did you expect?*

"Did you... with him?" I asked.

"We had many a passionate encounter," Miss Wandilyn said wistfully, "But he continued to forget me afterwards."

"Guys do that," I said in apology, "Doesn't matter what our species is."

"It was special!" she shouted.

"I suppose considering what your father did to you, I can't be surprised that you're a little... left field."

For the first time the gun grip wavered a little, "What do you mean, 'what my father did to me?'"

"I mean just that, actually."

"Must you turn everything into some kind of call back joke or pithy anecdote?" Edna groaned, "It gets so tiresome!"

I was about to respond but Miss Wandilyn said, "My *father* never *did* anything to me. I did it to him. I wanted him."

"Well..." I said tentatively, "Also, I meant to ask, centaurs are a different species aren't they?.... Your assassin friend tapped bestiality but you've added incest and bestiality together in only a couple of pages, it's pretty impressive."

"We won't be judged by a man like you," she said.

"So it's 'we' now?" I asked, "A moment ago it was just you. Tell me, was it scripted that Edna should have to be penetrated by a horse penis?"

173

"Don't bother trying that route detective," Edna said, "Aggregosh was a fierce and powerful lover. They say the centaurs are the last lovers you'll ever want."

"Or be able to have," I said, "Both of you have privates about as tight as a pair of sleeping bags."

Miss Wandilyn opened her mouth to say something, decided otherwise, closed it and shot me.

It is possible to avoid a bullet. Morei Ueshiba, the founder of Aikido, once said that in battle during the war he was able to see the line of fire coming from guns, allowing him to avoid them in the same way we would avoid laser sights if we could see them. This talent made him invincible when facing combatants because he was able to see their approach and thereby redirect it. This same training had been drummed into us at school and during those long periods of hard training where, after days of being kept awake and training we were then challenged to survive. It is during periods like this that you discover a bow and arrow can be far more dangerous than a gun in the right hands. A gun requires a finger squeezing the trigger which is an active decision to shoot, whereas a bow just requires the string to be released and that is merely a decision to release. There is a world of difference between those two decisions. I digress, which I apologise for, but the reason for my digression is that while I spotted the line of fire which was aiming for my chest I had assumed that Miss Wandilyn would have been a better shot. I am not a gun man, I know very little about guns, I do not recognise them I do not like them so any make or design mentioned would have been guesswork, but the gun was one of the bigger ones because the recoil was such that the gun flew up and out of her hands like a cat stuck with a cattle prod. This changed the direction of the barrel at the very last minute and the bullet, which was aimed for my belly, hit me with remarkable precision in the forehead.

16.

Across from the table a very well dressed gentleman kept scraping his fork against the glass plate as he tried to spear one of the olives. He realised that I was staring and sheepishly put down the knife and fork saying, "I can always come back to it I suppose,"

He was an elderly gent, with light blue eyes, backswept salt and pepper hair and a face dominated by high cheekbones and a pointy chin. The lines around his eyes were sentences that spoke of seeing it all, hearing it all and knowing it all.

"You're Satan, aren't you?" I asked, pointing at him.

He shifted happily in his seat, turning his head slightly to one side and frowning, "That was quicker than I expected." he said.

I shrugged and looked around the restaurant, "Hold on, I know this place. This is that Spanish club/bar down from Bank Plain isn't it?"

Satan picked up the olive with his fingers and popped it into his mouth. He followed my gaze around and said, "I believe it is."

"So we're still in Norwich?"

"Norwich is Purgatory," Satan reminded me.

"So I am dead," I said, gingerly fingering my forehead where I was certain there should have been a hole. There wasn't one but I felt that there should have been, like that first time you go to the clinic and get the scrape and for hours afterwards you're wondering if that nurse maybe left something up there. I checked my suit quickly; at least I had died looking good.

"You're not dead," Satan said, his expression tightening as if he hated to point out the obvious.

"I got shot in the head," I said, "I hope I'm dead. So where is your skivvy, the devil I made the deal with at the crossroads? I was expecting to see him pick me up."

Satan chewed on his olive for a moment, not once breaking his eye contact with me. He swallowed and wiped his mouth with a napkin and as soon as he put it onto the plate a waitress in a white shirt and a black tie picked it up and left.

"When I found out about the deal I decided to come and pay you a visit myself,"

Satan said, then added in a reprosit tone, "Oh don't worry, he will still get the commission, but I wanted to see you for myself."

I recognised the feel of a tumbler in my hand and brought the drink of rum to my lips, it was very good, I asked, "I thought you weren't able to come up to Purgatory?"

"Are you a theologian?"

"I've had a vested interest of late,"

"Well... it's all a bit of a business," he said, "My business mostly. I am just the CEO and Managing Director of Hell, just a member of the board. I can go wherever I like but you know how it is, work keeps you so busy - I've not had a chance to get out of the office for about two thousand years."

"You're a slave to your work," I remarked.

"Precisely, the chains of perdition are nothing more than a contract I signed a long time ago."

"I know the contract wasn't with God," I said, "I've met him."

The king of devils, the fallen angel, smiled. It was the kind of smile that made you want to be on his side, because you'd hate to see it if you weren't, "I know. Lilith and I are fairly close too."

I drummed the table with my fingertips and asked, wanting to keep the conversation moving to my rhythm, "Why in this restaurant?"

"Have you ever noticed how busy this place is despite it having the worst service in the city?" Satan asked.

"Yes."

"It is where we direct all the fresh souls entering Norwich," he said.

I looked around, "Can they see me?"

"Of course," he said.

I caught the eye of a waitress and held up my empty glass and nodded my head to the man opposite me. In less than a minute I had a fresh drink in front of me, I saluted Satan and said, "Nice."

Satan looked frustrated, I asked if he was okay.

"This isn't going to script," he explained, "You're making it very difficult for me to get to the point."

"I've been told I do that."

"It's like you're following your own dialogue in your head," he continued. "Don't you want to know why you're here?"

"I died,"

"No you didn't,"

"Well that could be awkward then," I said, drinking my rum. "People will get really annoyed if I can take a bullet to the head and still enjoy my rum."

Satan sighed and beckoned the waitress for a drink.

I made myself comfortable. "So tell me about yourself Satan, I've heard so much about you. Do you prefer Satan or Lucifer? Or any of the other names you like?"

His drink arrived and he downed it in a single bounce of his Adam's apple and asked for another. "You can call me whatever you like," he said, "I shouldn't be surprised about this, I've heard a lot about you over the years."

"You're a fan are you?" I chuckled.

Ignoring the last, he accepted the next drink with gratitude and put it on the table in front of him. He took a breath and said, "I'm going to explain to you why you are here and then I'm going to tell you something that you don't know and it will come as a shock. May I ask that you just sit there and drink your rum without speaking?"

I ordered another drink, with a snap of my fingers, smiled gallantly, "You got it."

"Excellent," Satan said. "Where to begin. You are here because the devil who saved you from the winchikari believed that he was getting the best deal of his career and made a bit of a song and dance about it. I'm afraid to say that he has gotten a little bit in his own way with regards to you delivering the soul of the assassin to him, especially as he wanted the forfeit of your soul. This is impossible as that is quite a valuable thing."

I was going to ask something but he gave me a look that made my lips curl around my teeth and my tongue to roll backwards on itself.

"The *reason* your soul is valuable is due to your skillset. Your Schooling in South Africa has made you formidable both in combat and stealth - but you have also combined these talents into a form of natural luck. You luck out more than others. It is confounding to perceive, almost as if you are written to survive.

"Like any business we keep an eye on specifically talented people, there are many uses for a man such as yourself and for a long time we had planned to recruit you. Oh, don't look at me like that, ours is a Hell of a business and not all of it is fire and brimstone; have you any concept at all of how many different levels of afterlife I am involved with? I *always* recruit the brightest and the boldest... besides, Heaven is *boring*." He drank some of his drink and put the glass down, "Where was I? Yes! So we had planned to recruit you, probably in acquisitions, the money there is fantastic and the perks are renowned. But we missed the opportunity."

"The Embassy?" I asked.

He let that interruption slide with just a warning glance. "Yes, they got in the way of things. But it was what happened before that to which I refer."

I had no idea what he was talking about.

"Tell me, do you remember what you were doing before you worked for the Norwich City Council's Embassy for the Lost, Late and Otherwise?"

I waited to make sure that if I answered he wouldn't make my face fold itself again. He prompted me on, "I was selling timeshare in Tenerife,"

He smiled, "Yes, that was a promising start really. We have a steady stem of timeshare salesmen coming through my way... so tell me

Donnie, how did you go from selling timeshare to working for the Embassy?"

Not quite sure what he was getting at I explained: I had made a lot of money in Tenerife selling over-priced timeshare to people who wouldn't be able to enjoy it, namely married couples and old aged pensioners. Not only had the money been good but since the company I worked with insisted all the salesmen use aliases instead of their real names I was able to enjoy an expensive lifestyle without anyone from School finding me. I had only come to Norwich after the bottom fell out of the market and a lot of us lost our positions. Sunday night we had celebrated as millionaires and come Monday morning we were told we didn't have a job, accommodation or a future. Penthouse apartment to sleeping on a hill within a space of twenty four hours ... I had come to Norwich then and worked a number of remedial jobs until finding a shoebox under my bed.

"I do find it humorous that they let you choose your title and position so easily," Satan said with a chuckle, "It's like watching a child play. You've got the body of a warrior, the intelligence of a genius and the mental focus of a five year old.

But there is a big part of it which you can't remember can you?"

"Enlighten me then?"

He smiled, "Be careful, Adam and Eve asked me to do that before and look what happened to them."

"Please," I said.

"You know how Norwich makes use of the Late?" he enquired.

"Of course," I said, "They work."

"More to the point they are given employment," Satan said, "These are souls who have not achieved anything great, their karma is low. They haven't stood for anything of worth and have merely continued as a cog in the consumerist nature of their lives... they are not evil and so they cannot be punished but they are not glorious. So, they are given a wage and they work in offices, they work in businesses, accounting, administration. You see them walking the streets in their work suits every day, getting old but you don't realise that they're already dead. They don't realise it either, they go back to their homes in the evening, they watch television, they eat food, they engage in their hobbies and what they think is 'life' goes on for them. But they don't know that they are dead because they cannot remember the moment of their death. This is why we have haunted houses and ghosts, spectres and spirits floating around. These are people who don't know that they are dead and so they grow angry, they're not given work and so like vagrants, they haunt and are ignored. These are the Lost."

"I know this," I said.

He sighed, put his elbows onto the table, closed his eyes and pinched the skin between his eyebrows, "Do you remember dying Don?"

"Well I did just get shot in the head," I said, "But you said I hadn't died!"

"I said you weren't dead," he said.

"You just asked if I remembered dying?!" I cried out.

"You didn't die tonight, you died long before you came to Norwich. You were very well hung Don."

My fresh glass of rum was halfway to my lips, but it went down to the table without completing the journey: it touched the table top with a pronounce clunk.

"Say again?"

"You don't remember. The School found you in Tenerife, at the time you were sleeping on the hill top overlooking Los Christianos. Do you remember it?"

I did. It doesn't rain in Tenerife, nor are there any real animals that live there aside from what the tourists bring, mostly cockroaches, cats and the odd dog. This meant roughing it on the hill is a very simple process. When I lost my apartment I climbed a hill to get to a spot half way up where someone had put out a pair of sun loungers. This had been for lovers who were in the know wanting to get a breath-taking view while enjoying their "holiday frollick" I had slept on those sun loungers, using the clothes from my suitcase as blankets for a week.

"What happened after that week?" Satan asked, "In that coffee house?"

Of course I remembered the coffee house. I had gone there every day since losing my job. After the company I had worked for had refused to pay me my last wage (because in all fairness they didn't have the money for it), I had budgeted the last euros into how much coffee I could get. The last day I was on the island I had been sitting in the corner table and the barista at the counter had given me a free coffee and a sandwich. It had been the best meal I had ever tasted. That same morning a friend I had known from the office had passed the store and seen me hiding in the corner. Thanks to his wife having "family" money he had been in a better position than me. Thanks to him I got a shower that night, a big meal and a plane ticket to Norwich. From that day onwards everything seemed to go alright, I flitted from job to job but every job opened more doors, every opportunity gave me more and through it all I just seemed to cruise happily and unchanged.

After explaining this Satan nodded sympathetically, "On the last night on that hill, one of your classmates from School was sent to collect a contract on you. He was contracted to bring your head back with him, either attached to your body so that they could make use of your talents as a graduate or unattached so that you could be an example to others. It was a fierce battle and you managed to kill him."

"I did?" I asked, "How?"

"I'm not entirely fluent with the language of the attacks, but even if you hadn't thrown him head first down the hillside he would never have walked or talked properly again."

"So I won?"

"But you weren't happy with the victory, you knew that they would keep coming after you for the rest of your life, you knew that there would never be any peace and that the fight would never be won. You wanted that victory, you wanted to steal it from them. You found rope, six feet of it, fashioned a noose and hung yourself in an abandoned chapel at the top of the hill."

"Bullshit," I said.

"Do I need to fold your tongue again?" he snapped. "As I said I am explaining why you are here! Your suicide was not born out of depression, sadness or loss. It was born out of a sense of victory and spite, you had to win at any costs. But a suicide is a suicide and of all the souls in all of the universe the only ones guaranteed a place in Hell are suicides."

"So you are here to collect?"

"I swear I will rip your tongue out if you interrupt me when I'm making my climatic end," he threatened. Sullenly, I shank into my seat and he continued, "However, there were mediating factors to consider. If you were labelled a suicide I would not be able to use you, it's like a school employing a registered sex offender. Suicides are difficult to work with, I would have lost you... when you made that decision on that hill, you would have used any means necessary. You would have thrown yourself down the hill, you would have slit your wrists, you would have drowned yourself. I had to give you an avenue that you would use and would keep you within my grasp. Luckily, I am known for my contracts and I am always aware of the loopholes."

It dawned on me then.

"Exactly," Satan said, "I gave you the rope... and knowing that there were no real trees nearby I knew you would find that abandoned building and do it there... It was a neat job and efficient. But you had no idea what you had done."

Leaning on the table, hungry to hear more, I gestured for him to continue.

"One of the loopholes in the life contract, one that is seldomly available is The Nooseman Clause. Have you heard of it?"

I hadn't.

"Suicides are usually given a place as slaves and servants, they didn't value their lives and so they won't be valued in death. Circus workers, sewer workers and call centre staff are usually suicides. It is a horrible life of being undervalued. But," here he held up a finger, "With the Nooseman Clause, whenever someone is hung by the neck in a place of holy worship without their final rites being given their soul becomes entwined with the very rope that does the job. This is across the board including suicides, mob lynchings, executions and all religions and faith. You, Donnie Rust, are a Nooseman."

I sat back and looked at my hands. Beyond the cuffs of my shirt I could see the indented pores of my flesh, those little scars that kids pick up on their knuckles and fingers, sowed freckles on the skin.

"You are a halfie," Satan continued, "You live but only because your rope binds your soul to your body. And whoever controls the rope controls you."

"Like a slave?" I asked meekly.

He pressed his lips together. When he spoke again his voice held an apologetic undertone, "It was this or a call centre in Diss," he said, "You didn't deserve that and frankly you were too important. You can imagine, hangings in holy places aren't that frequent anymore and when they are it is seldom with people of your skillset."

I felt like the air had been taken from me, I stared at the remaining rum in my glass, trying to let it all seep in.

"So, who has my rope?"

"The Embassy," Satan explained, "This is why they don't care whether you play Ambassador or detective because you already have another title. I'm not happy about this, my intention was to get the rope for myself but the Embassy already had an agent in the field. That bloody work colleague of yours and his bitch of a wife with all her family wealth."

"Ha, the ticket to Norwich."

"Precisely. Fortunately, I'm very patient. While I was not allowed to make contact with you while you were in Norwich I knew you would eventually make a deal with a devil - and so you did. You getting shot was a bit of a surprise though but there is a process to go through and I was able to stretch things out a little by meeting you here. Loopholes and all that."

"But I feel human," I said, "I've always said I was human. The whole city considers me human."

"You called yourself the Ambassador as well," he said, "You then changed that to detective. Titles don't matter. You are what you are. If you want proof, ask yourself why you don't need to eat? Food for you was always just about calorie intake, whereas you drank coffee and alcohol because you *loved* them. You don't need to eat, drink or sleep but you do these things out of habit. Your physical responses are all part of the deal. Suicides don't remember their deaths and think they are alive; their hearts beat, their body ages, their wounds heal, they get older, but they are no more alive than a heart outside the body being kept alive with machines."

It was all getting a little more complicated for me.

"The School think I'm alive," I pointed out.

"So does most of the world," he countered, "What does it matter? You can't die again unless you untie your rope."

"You want it don't you?" I asked.

"Of course I do," he said with a grin, "But as I said I am very patient. You are not separate from the universe and you are still aging. What happens when you get so old that you cannot remember who you are, that your mind fades and all that you're left with is an old and feeble body?"

"I don't know,"

"Nothing," he said, this time with a wholly different smile. Satan's evil was not illustrated in horns or a forked tongue, but in one, solitary smile, it was a smile that chilled the air around it, "You won't die. One day you will hundreds of years old, your body will be dry and brittle like autumn leaves, your mind as burnt out as overbaked bread- you would have lost everything that makes you you... the Embassy won't have any use for you. But I will. I know all of the loop holes and when all you want to do is die, I will be there to make sure you don't."

It was my time to smile, "Well," I said, taking a sip, "At least I know where we stand."

Satan agreed, "Now, I believe that you have a soul to give us."

17.

"He is still breathing, shoot him again."

I was aware of a number of impacts in my chest, each one so jarring and hard, sending ripples across my whole body so that I couldn't count them and they only ended when the gun started clicking against an empty magazine. There was a pause; a sensation of someone pressing a hand against my throat.

"Oh for God's sake this is getting ridiculous," Miss Wandilyn said.

"It's going to get worse," I said, opening my eyes.

There was a surprised shriek and the gun hit me in the head. I covered my face with my hands and muttered nasally, "You *threw* the gun at me?"

"Why aren't you dead?!" Miss Wandilyn shouted.

Carefully I pushed myself to my feet, repeating in my mind that the fiery, ripping, tearing screaming pain in my torso was just in my head and that the hole in my forehead was not as bad as it felt. Strangely, while the pain in my skull was horrible I couldn't feel the bullet in my head. The brain having no ability to feel anything - *All in my head, all in my head, all in my head.*

Once standing I said, "It's a bit of a story I'm afraid. Not entirely sure it's true either, given the source of it."

Both women were openly staring at me, more specifically at a point just above my eyes. Gingerly I prodded the flesh with my fingers and found what they were looking at. There was a hole, no bigger than a five pence piece, right in my head. Rigid around the edges like a puncture hole in calabash, I was aware of liquid running down my neck and with a slight uncomfortable wince I reached behind my head and found where the bullet had exited.

"Holy cow," I muttered as I found a hole big enough for my fist to fit in. Muggy, jelly-like brains hung in tatters from this gaping cavern in the back of my head. I looked at Edna, whose mouth was hanging open, and asked, "Where is the bathroom?"

Blinking, the shirime demon pointed to a door adjacent to the elevator entrance. I excused myself and went to check myself in the mirror. Firstly I checked the front of my face. The bullet had hit my forehead with such a velocity that it had entered it with a small polite hole. The back of my skull was another matter, about where a Jewish man would wear his kippah was a hole about the same size. I checked my torso and saw the wounds there, similarly small but bleeding heavily.

I felt alive. I could feel the pain, the heart beat - that was one thing. But I could also think. I quickly said the alphabet as fast as I could, recited the nine times table and sung the first verse of Sweet Child of Mine by Guns and Roses. I had coordination within my body to tie my shoelaces, and I could even do some jumping jacks, while, all the same, lacking the brains in my skull to be able to do any of this.

"Well this is odd," I said.

Buttoning my shirt up and straightening my tie I went back into the apartment and found that Miss Wandilyn and Edna were sitting on the stools at the kitchen counter, smoking. Joining them it was the shirime who asked.

"What the hell are you?"

"A Nooseman," I said, prodding the fleshy exposed brain at the top of my head, "Don't worry it's all still pretty new to me. Aren't we fighting anymore?"

Miss Wandilyn said, "If I'm honest it's all come as a bit of a shock. Do you mind if we just take a break for a moment?"

I didn't mind. I pulled up the stool on the opposite side of the counter and sat down. I had a very strange sensation of coolness spreading through my skull.

Edna was staring at my forehead.

"Would you mind not staring?" I asked.

"I can see light coming through your head," she said fast, "It's… distracting."

Miss Wandilyn offered me one of the cigarettes and I accepted, I lit it up and took a long drag, "Bit of a day,"

Edna got off the stool and started making some coffee

"I've heard of Noosemen," Miss Wandilyn said, "Dad used to speak of them all the time. Explains why he liked you so much."

"He could have mentioned it to me," I said, "It would have saved a lot of trouble. Seeing as we're not fighting anymore, are you going to let Danielle go?"

"I don't see why not," Wandilyn said. She looked over her shoulder at the blood on the floor and the very large splatter of it, combined with bone shards against the pillar, "But I think I'll clean this place up first. But what happens now? You know that I won't be arrested."

"I'll report back to Gregore and let him know who is to blame, he can try and find you," I said, "Good luck to him. I do have a question, why did you have Edna kill your dad?"

"I am a jealous woman," Miss Wandilyn said, "He was one of the only people who knew I existed and he was sleeping with other women. A lot of women, like hundreds of them. It was like rape, because they couldn't remember him afterwards so he was getting away with it. That didn't even bother me that much it was that he was losing interest in me... it hurt..."

I was about to say something consoling when she added, "Also it was great for the show, the viewer ratings went through the roof afterwards."

Edna brought us our coffees and went back to where she was sitting. We drank them in silence, avoiding each other's eyes. Occasionally there was a wet drip as I leaked onto the kitchen floor.

"This is all my fault," the shirime finally said.

"Oh don't say that," I muttered cruelly, "We were all happy blaming Wandilyn here."

Beseechingly the shirime looked at me, "Did you not wonder why the winchikari attacked you and Danielle in the taxi?"

"It had crossed my mind," I lied.

"When your ogre friend killed my sister, I made a deal with a devil, I wanted revenge on you, I wanted to castrate you *so badly,* I didn't even hesitate to agree with him. He said that I was to kill three people for Miss Wandilyn and that the third would be you. Miss Wandilyn had taken me to Aggregosh's tent before to keep me unnoticed that first time when I took his mighty, meaty, horse penis so I knew the way. I had been following you, using the gaps and helping Miss Wandilyn keep tabs on you. I was hiding in the taxi's boot when it attacked you. That's why it found you and me in the city."

"That was great for the viewership," Miss Wandilyn said offhandedly, "Unexpected, but I checked the statistics before I came here."

"What happens if you don't get to kill me?" I asked.

"Kill two and the third will be you," she said, "The contract isn't completed until it's done."

"You killed two other people?" I asked.

Perhaps it's because of my reputation for being an idiot, but Edna just seemed frustrated. She slapped the counter top and said, "Yes, I killed Aggregosh and Jason Marcadius."

I leant back, both hands on the counter and said, "Thank you Edna."

"For what?" she asked.

"Well I also made a deal with a devil," I said, pulling out an envelope from my inner jacket pocket, "It's all in here."

Casually I put it onto the counter top and pushed it forward for her to see.

Scowling, she picked up the envelope and looked inside and I think she realised a second later what was happening because her face crinkled in rage and she leapt up at me, sending the stool flying out behind her. But she didn't make it across the counter to rip out my throat because from the floorboards beneath her came an explosion of black tendrils, so dark and black they were two dimensional and they struck the shirime with such force that Miss Wandilyn was thrown sideways.

These tendrils wrapped around Edna's wrists and ankles, holding her aloft.

I staggered backwards until I hit the stove, my eyes wide.

The Deal Devil appeared with Satan himself standing nearby. The CEO of Hell stepped aside, gesturing with a sweep of his hand for the Deal Devil to do his thing, and the smoky creature, still immaculately dressed, stepped forward and addressed me in a begrudging tone:

"Thank you for completing your contract with me," he said, "This will bring our contract to a close however I have been authorized to give you the choice to save this creature's soul. She was merely avenging her sister's death a notable and worthy act and her contract completes with your castration, an event that as has been recently demonstrated that you would survive. If you allow her to complete her contract then we can consider this matter closed."

Satan was standing near the wall, his hands clasped rather respectfully in front of him, totally poker faced.

"Will these wounds heal?"

"Wounds will heal," the Deal Devil said, his voice carrying over Edna's screams, "But nothing removed grows back."

"You killed my sister!" Edna cried, "You condemned her to a long and painful death, you deserve this vengeance and you know it!"

Miss Wandilyn had regained her composure and was standing out of the way, following her natural instincts to dissolve into the background. I looked at her movement and wondered if any of those present would remember her.

"What about Miss Wandilyn?" I asked Satan.

"Who?" he asked.

I looked at the forgettable woman as she flattened her back against the wall, our eyes met and I said simply, "You owe me."

She left via the elevator, which nobody noticed.

"Have you gone mad?" the Deal Devil asked, "Who are you talking to?"

"Nobody of importance," I said, off handed, "I am sorry Edna, but a deal is a deal and I like my bits."

The Deal Devil seemed overjoyed and he snapped his fingers with delight. Edna screamed the kind of scream that is screamed by someone who realises that this is it. The dark bonds that held her went taut and wound into a single thick stem with a snapping whip crack and bore her to the floorboards with a thump.

I leaned over the kitchen counter to watch as the shirime demon hit the floorboards buttocks first, and for a moment I didn't see what was happening but her screams changed pitch going from those of fear to those of agony. Seconds passed where nothing seemed to be happening, she was just sitting there screaming at the ceiling. She was sitting on a plug into hell, and hell was draining her. This was confirmed when, with an appropriately stomach turning sound of cracking bones and ripping tissues she was pulled inside out and dragged into Hell.

The Deal Devil vanished as politely as he had arrived and I was left in the room with Satan.

"Why did you do *that* to her?" I asked manically, "That was bloody horrible!"

Satan seemed nonplussed and beckoned me with a finger to join him outside on the balcony. The cool air hit me like a wall and I took in deep breaths while clinging to the banister.

"If you would care to take a look," he said pointing to the road that ran in front of the promenade in front of the building, "Over there."

I jerked at the sight of the winchakiri as it stood in the road waiting for me. Its black, stab wound eyes glaring at me.

"Oh for crying out loud," I sighed.

"Wait for it," he said at my side.

At that moment a swirling black hole the size of a bucket opened up above the demon, which looked up with marginal interest. Whatever fell from this hole was wet and dark, resembling the waste material of a butcher's and could be identified as chunky slop. It drenched the winchikari and the monster cried out into the night with a kind of elation that chilled me to my marrow. Its driver body flexed in happiness and it turned its horrid head up into the shower. When it was done the demon shook with pleasure and fell to the floor sucking at the mess on the floor, slurping it up off the asphalt. Once done it snuffled the ground looking for more, then rose and immediately departed.

"Please tell me that wasn't Edna," I said.

"Okay," Satan said, "If it makes it easier for you to deal with it. Oh don't be so soft Donnie, business is business after all. Here."

Moving faster than I expected he reached out and the coldest, iciest grip I've ever felt touched my head. It was so cold it blinded me for a second, the kind of deep, universal cold that nobody can be prepared for. He removed his hand and I fell over, gasping.

"Consider that a freebie," he said. He smiled that horrible smile again before, in a poof of whispered screams, he was gone.

I felt the back of my head and found that the hole had been replaced with skull, covered in scalp and in turn covered in hair. However a check in the mirror proved that my face was sporting a scar about the size of a five pence piece right in the middle of my forehead.

"Terrific," I said.

18.

Danielle had a cup of coffee ready for me when I arrived at the office the following morning.

"I understand that I have you to thank for my release from my kidnappers," she said matter-of-factly.

"I honestly couldn't say if I helped or not," I said.

"Nevertheless, thank you," she said, returning to her desk. She took out her iPad and started fingering it, "Seems that in my short absence you've made some interesting friends. An Inspector Box is waiting for you in the office."

Box stood to greet me as I closed the door behind me.

"The shirime demon who attacked you last year does have a sister," he said to me, "By the name of Edna Caristrange."

I thanked him, shook his hand and with infinite care and detail I told him everything about the case except for the actual facts and events. The crux of it was that I had found the killer and that she had been ingested by a winchakiri demon. I did however tell him the location of the brothel owned by the rakes and the events that were going on there. I also requested that he keep my name out of any reports and take all the credit for the find. He seemed pleased with this and eager for us to work together in the future.

As I bid goodbye to the Inspector, Danielle reminded me that the case wasn't entirely solved.

"Yes, the case was closed last night so I need to speak with Gregore."

"And there is also the other matter,"

"The other matter?" I asked.

At that moment there was the sound of hooves trotting down the street outside and a loud screeching voice from beyond, "Hey, Mister Detective, are you in there!?"

I sagged against the desk, "Oh Christ, Mary?"

Danielle shrugged and gave a serene smile, "A deal is a deal."

COMING SOON-

IN AND OUT OF WONDERLAND THROUGH THE
WHITE RABBIT'S HOLE.
(A Working Title)
By Donnie Rust

So to cut a long story short, it was Tuesday and I
was fighting a monster.

You may have recognised the sort; a tall and
lumbering patchwork of body parts sewn together
and reanimated through the power of lightning,
clever surgery and a reanimation serum. A serum
that had been stolen from Nicholas Flamel's
laboratory on Barner Street, although while I had
tried to explain this crime to the scientist
responsible, it was soon apparent that the man
had no idea what he was doing and while he may
have sewn the body parts together with a decent
understanding of anatomy and picked the perfect
night for a lightning storm to start howling at the
rain, it was the serum alone that had done the
trick.

This was probably why there was a hint of
surprise in his voice when he continued to cry,

"It's alive! It's alive?!" right up until the monster backhanded him with one of its misshapen hands and sent his head flying through the window and out into the street like a football.

I hasten to point out that the scientist's name was not Dr. Frankenstein but was as a matter of fact, Kevin. This seems important now, but was less so as the monster picked me up bodily in one of its hands and with a great wailing cry hurled me across the laboratory.

My fall was broken by a cabinet of chemicals which buckled under me as I crashed into it which upended shelves of chemicals and glass beakers over me.

"You absolute wanker!" I shouted, swiping at the chemicals that hissed and steamed across my lapels, "I have only just had this tailored!"

The monster screamed again. It was a horrid sound. Raspy and ear shredding – completely suited to a creature that looked like it had been put together by discounted spare parts. I clambered to my feet and turned to face it as it ran towards me, a haphazard endeavour as none of its limbs matched. At best it clambered forward on three of its limbs, trailing power cables and tubing.

Lightning flashed outside, painting the laboratory and all its horrors in bleached white light and the rage and anguish within the monster's eyes shone out of its sockets as it swiped at me with a hand. I avoided the strike by ducking under it, pawing the leathery forearm and redirecting the force of the blow, managing to misdirect the creature off balance and send it hurtling, like an avalanche of meat into yet another shelf of beakers.

Kevin, while not possessing a shred of credible scientific reasoning, had certainly made up for it in commitment to the role.

His laboratory was a rat's maze of shelves bedecked with vials and long coiling loops of tubing connecting bubbling beakers of colourful chemicals. Above us a lightning conductor rod of iron and copper wire buzzed disconcertingly and thick cables snaked across the floor bundled together with shoelaces.

The monster thrashed and howled with inconsolable rage as it struggled to get to its feet and took to throwing beakers of acid at me.

My phone started buzzing merrily in my jacket pocket and I took shelter behind a large porcelain tub filled with fowl smelling ammonia while glass beakers sailed over my head.

"Hello?"

"Are you done yet?" my personal assistant asked.

"Danielle?" I said, peeking over the rim of the tub as the monster was tugging at the long wires from its back that had tangled around the shelves, "What the hell are you still doing awake?"

"It's a full time job with you," she muttered, "And I get paid overtime so it's okay."

I sat down against the side of the tub, "I pay you overtime? We didn't discuss this?"

"Do you want me to go?" she asked.

"Well," I said, getting up and peeking again, "I am having a bit of a – shit."

The monster was gone. Cables overhead spasmed and offloaded a shower of sparks onto the destroyed shelves, bloody cables snaked and coiled malevolently as they sought for their monster which was, against all reason, gone.

"I *beg your pardon?*" Danielle said with great indignation, "Are you on the toilet?"

"No," I whispered into the phone looking left and right and behind me, "I'm at Kevin's laboratory fighting his fucking monster."

"He succeeded?" her voice was heady with incredulousness.

"Thanks to Nick's serum," I said, "But I'm afraid Kevin is lacking a head..."

Kevin's body was missing. Through the broad factory windows the lightning flashed revealing a large puddle of blood with no body lying in it and mismatched footprints leading away from it.

"Terrific," I muttered, "Danielle, how do I kill the monster?"

"Bear with," she said, her voice echoing as she put me on loudspeaker, "I'm just searching now."

"You don't know?"

"I'm trying to find out be patient,"

The darkness around me was so thick it could have been made of black velvet curtains. In it chains hanging from the ceiling rattled ominously, water dripped and even the sparking pylons didn't penetrate the blackness. But inside it there was the sound of labored breathing; wet, angry and hateful.

"Danielle..." I urged.

"Okay, okay, the elixir – sorry- serum of Nicholas Flamel can grant life, in large enough amounts even grant immortality. How much was the monster given?"

Somewhere in the darkness I heard a wet crunching sound that made me think of a burrito with chicken bones being crushed in a mulsher: the unique sound creating by a combination of wet flesh being perforated and bones being split.

"All of it," I said, "I imagine all of it."

"Set it on fire and then cut off its head," she said, "Only way."

"In that order?"

"You can try it the other way if you feel the need?"

An ear shredding screech from my left flank made me jump and the monster bounded from the darkness with stringy remains of Kevin hanging from its broken and mismatched teeth. Blood spilled from the gaps in its cheeks where the skin had sealed over what had been decomposing flesh and its combination bloodshot and egg yolk yellow eyes were wild with destructive anger.

I screamed and threw my phone at it. The small device hit the monster directly on the tip of its bullish nose. The creature flinched, its eyes half closing with surprise. It skidded to a halt, blinking. A lightning flash caught us both in a perfect picture, my staring at the creature in abject terror barely daring to breath and the creature standing just as still with its face depicting the mental processes involving 'tip of the nose' pain for the first time.

Then, all at once, the monster flung its hands up to its face so suddenly that it lost its balance, spun once and fell forward onto its face. It then began to cry.

All things considered, I prefer anger rather than sorrow, I don't know how to deal with crying and after an appropriate time of gawping at this gigantic quilt of body parts trembling and wailing into the floor I backed away. I remembered my phone at the last minute and carefully retrieved it, as I reached down to collect it from beside the monster it froze and its face, turned ever more horrific given the number of different facial expressions that it held, beheld me for a moment.

I was close enough now that it could have taken my head off with a single swipe, but instead it recoiled from me and my phone. Its cries were childlike, the screaming howls of an infant born against its will, given life as a half opened package. The only way to answer such cries would be to wrap this monster up in a towel and stick it to a mother's tit. Which gave me an immediate idea, I called Danielle back.

"Are you alive?"

"As alive as I can be," I pointed out, "But so is the monster. I can't burn it though," I said.

"Why not?" she asked, "The contract says either find the elixir or destroy it. Nicholas can make more but he doesn't want it falling into the wrong hands!"

"Thank you for pointing that out," I said, "I'm sure the readers are happy to know that little twist. But I have an idea."

"Oh hell," she muttered, "You really have to stop having ideas."

"Why?" I asked.

The monster looked up again and I cleared about six feet in a single surprised skip. It glared at me, its eyebrows dancing at the current of thought, its blackened lips worked, its blue steak tongue snaking out and getting in the way of its teeth before it managed to shape a word, "*Why?*"

"Oh my God," I said to it, "You can talk?"

"*Why?*" it asked again, it's face twisting and contorting into a corpse smile of delight, it took a breath and said:

"*Why? Whywhywhywhywhy!*"

It then sprang to its feet, spread its hands and started dancing around merrily, flinging it's limbs willy nilly and spinning with delight shouting at the top of its mismatched lungs,
"Whywhywhywhywhywhywhywhywhy!"
I closed my mouth and said into the phone, "Okay I see your point,"

ALSO BY DONNIE RUST
GODHUNTER: BOOK ONE OF THE DAEMON
SERIES.

In a world where everyone seems to have a
reason Rayne Ensley feels like she is lost until she
manages to capture an elusive and ferocious
vigilante on camera. Overnight she becomes an
internet sensation and her world is irrefutably
changed. However, while enjoying superstardom
in the adult film industry and being romanced by
the wealthiest of men she is also hunted by an
immortal responsible for a long series of grizzly
justice killings.

Available in paperback on Amazon.

Printed in Great Britain
by Amazon

82401873R00129